A Chris to Remember

By

T S James

Acknowledgements

To my beloved wife.

This book is filled with the magic and warmth of the Christmases we've spent together. May your joy and enthusiasm for Christmas always brighten our lives. Whether it's watching Christmas films in July or listening to carols on the radio, your spirit keeps the heart of Christmas alive all year round.

This book, '*A Christmas to Remember,*' is dedicated to you. May this remind you of my love for you, and to a lot more Christmases together.

Additionally, I must express my sincere appreciation to Publish Nation. Their expertise, patience and help in bringing this book to fruition, has been a thoroughly enjoyable experience.

And finally, to my Beta-readers, your input and comments have helped shape this book enormously. I cannot thank you all enough, you have been an invaluable part of my editing.

'*May you NEVER be too old to believe in the magic of Christmas.*'

Prologue

In the shadow of ancient woods and nestled among rolling hills, there's a village called Santclausby, once brimming with magic and a strong sense of community. It wasn't always known by this enchanting name; once, it was called Yuleton, a simple place of cottages and winding lanes where each Christmas, the air sparkled with a special kind of enchantment. Many centuries ago, during a particularly bitter winter, the snow piled so high it buried doorways and the cold bit deep into every home. It was then that a mysterious old traveller arrived. He wore a bright red coat and brought a sack full of hand-carved toys and magical trinkets for the children. As he left, his footprints in the snow glowed under the moonlight, spreading tales of wonder throughout Yuleton.

Year after year, the traveller returned, each visit adding more magic. He decorated the village's Christmas tree with twinkling, enchanted ornaments and left behind sparkling ice sculptures of woodland creatures that glistened in the winter sun. His visits transformed Yuleton into a realm of ceaseless marvel, a place where the spirit of giving and the magic of Christmas thrived. Years later, he gifted a villager with a magical lantern and a scroll. Following his instructions, they renamed the village Santclausby and learned to summon the wonderful ice sculptures every Christmas, keeping the traveller's legacy alive.

As the village grew famous, artisans and craftsmen came to live there, each adding their own touch of Christmas magic. The main square boasted a grand Christmas tree, and the Magic Ice Sculpture Garden became a marvel. But over time, things changed. Younger generations moved away, drawn by the excitement of city life. The once vibrant celebrations dwindled, and the magical ice sculptures became just memories, their stories buried under snow.

Now, on this 12th of December, as the village awakes under a heavy sky, the festive spirit that once defined Santclausby feels as distant as a warm summer. Amidst this forgotten cheer, two young girls, Lily and Sophie, find themselves in the school playground, grappling with the true essence of Christmas magic. Their story mirrors the village's own tale of fading wonders and forgotten joys. Santclausby, with its now quiet streets and lost legends, hides a deeper mystery waiting to be rediscovered. As we journey through the pages of this story, we'll uncover the village's secrets, revisit its history, and perhaps rekindle its long-lost spirit. For hidden in every whispered legend and seen in every hopeful child's eyes, is a path leading back to the enchantment that once danced through Santclausby.

This is the beginning of our tale, a story of enchantment and reclaimed wonder, waiting just for you to turn the page.

Chapter 1

In the village of Santclausby, where Christmas was once celebrated with love and joy. A silent frost has now settled over its charm. Gone are the vibrant celebrations that painted the village in festive hues; in their place, a quiet nostalgia whispers through the streets. Where laughter and jingling bells once filled the air, now only faint memories linger. The famous Magic Ice Sculpture Garden, once a testament to the village's creativity and joy, seems nothing more than a fairy tale buried under layers of snow. Santclausby used to be a magical place, a true Christmas wonderland. Artisans at the Christmas market sparkled with joy, weaving happiness into the very essence of village life. But those bright days have faded. Now, the grand Christmas tree in the village square, once a beacon of light and cheer, stands forlorn, its branches drooping under the weight of the snow, bereft of lights and ornaments.

The local church, which echoed with songs and festive laughter, now resounds with the hollow silence of a dwindling congregation. The spirit of unity and shared celebration has slowly ebbed away, leaving behind an emotional longing for the Christmases of old. In Santclausby, the echo of Christmas past calls softly, waiting for new joy to awaken its slumbering streets.

The school playground whispered with tales of the past and future hopes that linger in the frosty air.

Here, Lily, a fiery red-haired girl, eyes as deep and green as emeralds, sat perched on an old wooden bench. Her pink scarf and matching bobble hat, a soft, warm comparison to the cold surrounding whiteness, nodded gently in the crisp breeze. Around her, the school playground was alive with the echoes of children, their laughter and playful shouts an obvious contrast to the quiet melancholy of the village.

With a pen clutched between her small, determined fingers, Lily meticulously inked her Christmas desires onto the pages of her diary. Each word, an indication of her belief in the magic of the season, her breath danced in puffs clouding in the chill of the air. In the dwindling spirit of the village, she stood as all

1

young children do, a true believer in Christmas and in Santa Claus. Her vivid imagination shining brightly as a guiding star, illuminating the joy and wonder of the festive season.

Then, as gently as the first snowfall, Sophie approached. Her voice, a delicate chime against the wintry stillness, broke into Lily's concentration, "Hi Lily, what are you doing?" she asked, her curiosity wrapped in the soft layers of her winter clothes.

Lily looked up, her face blooming into a smile. "I'm writing a letter to Santa! It's already December the 12th and I need to get it sent off." She replied, her voice a melody of innocence and excitement.

Sophie's expression shifted, a sombre note clouding her youthful features. "You know... he... doesn't really exist, right?" she said hesitantly, her voice low, carrying a weight which seemed too heavy for her young years.

The words hung in the air like a heavy cloud, casting a shadow of doubt over Lily's heart. "What? No way." said Lily incredulously. Her face changed as she contemplated Sophie's announcement. "What about all the gifts and the stories? And my letters!" Lily's voice wobbled, her pen shook a little in her hand.

Sophie let out a long breath, watching it fog up in the chilly air. "Well, my brother told me. He said he caught mum and dad sneaking presents under the tree." Her tone a mix of disappointment and reluctant knowing, "I asked mum if it was true, and... she said it was."

Lily's vibrant eyes widened in surprise, and at that moment, the innocence of her youth collided with this revelation. "But he's supposed to be real..." she whispered, more to herself than to Sophie, a mixture of confusion and betrayal swirling within her.

The playground, once a realm of joy and laughter, a scene from a happier time, now felt distant. Around them, the world seemed to pause; the trees appeared to lean in; the snowflakes halting their dance, as if the very earth itself held its breath, waiting for Lily's response. Lily's heart wavered, torn between the cherished stories of Santa's magic and the striking reality Sophie presented.

2

"I don't want to stop believing... It's all part of the Christmas magic." Lily's voice cracked slightly, the beginning of tears glistening in her eyes.

Sophie's eyes softened, touched by the weight of her revelation. "I'm sorry, Lily," she whispered, drawing near and giving her a gentle hug. "I didn't mean to upset you. Maybe... maybe there's still magic, just a different kind?"

Lily, shaken, but finding strength in her friend's embrace, looked up, her eyes shimmering with unshed tears, yet glinting with a growing resolve. "What kind of magic?" she asked, her voice soft but curious.

Sophie paused, her gaze wandering over the snow-draped playground. "Like the magic in our friendship, or just being there for each other," she offered softly.

Lily pondered as she blinked away her tears, considering Sophie's words. A small, brave smile broke through her sadness as she took Sophie's hand.

As they sat, surrounded by the serene beauty of the snowy day, Lily felt a shift within her. Turning her gaze from the unfinished letter to Santa, she embraced the warmth of Sophie's friendship. With a newfound determination, she looked back at Sophie; her smile resilient. "I think there's still some magic left for us to find. It's possible your brother doesn't know everything; perhaps Santa is more real than we think. "Sorry Sophie, but I think your mum and brother are wrong. There must be a Santa, and I will prove it."

Sophie looked at Lily and gave her a slight smile, "It would be great if you did, but..." Their conversation was interrupted as the bell rang out to end their break time. Lily's letter to Santa remained incomplete. Sophie slowly shook her head. 'Mum wouldn't lie to me,' she thought... 'she wouldn't.'

Sophie, her young face still holding the gravity of her her words, met Lily's earnest gaze with a touch of sadness, "I know it's hard to believe," she said gently, "but my mum said Santa isn't real, and she wouldn't lie to me, not about this."

Sophie's mother, known for her practical and realistic outlook on life, naturally held a sceptical view about the existence of Santa Claus. Her decision to share the truth with Sophie at the age of nine was influenced by her own upbringing and a strong desire to instil in her daughter the values of realism and gratitude.

Lily's heart ached with a mixture of disappointment and confusion. She looked down at her half-written letter, her small hand still gripping the pen as if it were a lifeline to the magical world she desperately wanted to hold on to.

"But, Sophie," she began, her voice tinged with hope, "I've always believed in him, and you did too, once... it can't just be made up, can it?"

Sophie's resolve wavered as she pondered Lily's words. She'd never seen Santa herself, but the stories, the twinkling lights, and the festive spirit of Christmas always made her heart swell with excitement. "Could it be the magic of Santa was real in a different way?" She bit her lip, torn between what she had been told and the enchanting world her friend still clung to.

Their thoughtful silence was broken by the clanging of the bell for a second time.

"Come on you two, time to come in!... break time is over!" shouted the teacher.

Lily's unfinished letter lay before her like an unanswered question. She sighed and began to pack her things back into her satchel. Her heart was burdened by the lingering enigma of Santa Claus.

Sophie watched her friend with a mix of sympathy and uncertainty.

"Mum wouldn't lie to me," she repeated softly, more to reassure herself than to convince Lily.

Later that day, Lily returned home from school with thoughts of Santa Claus swirling in her mind. She struggled to shake off the notion there was a deeper story than what Sophie's mother had revealed. That evening, after their kitchen had been transformed into a sweet-smelling haven of Christmas delights, and the aroma of freshly baked cookies filled the air, Lily decided it was time to confront her doubts. She summoned the courage to question her mother, who was busy baking their Christmas treats.

"Mum," Lily began hesitantly, her voice a soft murmur amidst the warmth of their cosy kitchen. Her mother turned to

4

her with a gentle smile, her flour-covered hands momentarily still. "What is it dear?"

Lily's emerald eyes met her mother's gaze, searching for answers to the question which had been weighing on her heart all day . "Is Santa Claus real?" she asked, her voice quivering with uncertainty.

Her mother's expression softened as she knelt down to Lily's eye level, she dusted off the flour before placing her hands on her daughter's shoulders. "Oh, Lily," she began, her voice filled with warmth and understanding, "Santa Claus is a bit like magic itself. He's not a person you can meet in the way we meet our friends, but he's very real in the way he brings joy, love, and kindness to the world during Christmas."

Lily listened intently, her heart yearning for the reassurance she sought. "But, Mum," she persisted, "what about the presents and the sleigh and the reindeer? Aren't they real?"

Her mother's eyes twinkled with a mix of nostalgia and love. "Well, sweetheart," she replied, "The presents and the joy they bring are very real. And as for the sleigh and the reindeer, they are symbols of the magic and wonder of Christmas. They remind us to be kind, generous, and to be full of love, just like Santa."

Her mum's words were comforting, and their reassurance brought a fleeting sense of relief to Lily's troubled heart. She knew her mother spoke with sincerity, but a seed of doubt still lingered within her.

Still not convinced Santa Claus was not real, Lily retreated to her room. She was unable to rid herself of the feeling that something crucial was missing, and the enchantment of Christmas had been tarnished.

Sitting at her dressing table, Lily gazed at her unfinished letter to Santa. The words she had written seemed like mere ink on paper, devoid of the belief which had once fuelled her Christmas wishes. She knew she had to make a choice, to continue doubting or to embrace the magic of Christmas, even if it meant not believing in something she once held so dear.

With a sigh, she carefully folded the letter, tucking it into a drawer. As she prepared for bed, her heart was heavy with uncertainty, but a small glimmer of hope remained. Sitting at her bedroom window, Lily watched as the snowflakes illuminated by the streetlight danced lazily outside her window, creating a picturesque winter scene. Each delicate flake pirouetted to the ground, settling into a glistening blanket of white velvet. It was a scene that, in previous years, would have filled Lily's heart with warmth and excitement. But now, there was only doubt. Lily's doubts in the existence of Santa Claus weighed heavily on her young shoulders. The enchantment of Christmas, once a magical season of wonder and anticipation, had, for now, lost its lustre for her.

It had all begun with a single sentence from her best friend Sophie, who had declared, with an air of authority. "Santa isn't real you know." Lily had scoffed at the idea initially, dismissing it as preposterous. Santa Claus had always been in her life, a symbol of joy and generosity, he had always been the symbol of Christmas.

But the seed of doubt had been planted, and it took root in Lily's mind. She reached a point where she could no longer ignore it. Like the growing snowbanks which lined the street outside her window, Lily's scepticism also grew. Lily climbed into bed and huddled under her quilt as she pondered this conundrum. Is it possible for one man to visit millions of homes in a single night, no matter how magical he might be? How can reindeer, however extraordinary, fly through the night sky carrying a sleigh full of presents? The joyous anticipation of Christmas, the once celebrated countdown to December 25th, was now replaced by a sense of sadness and loss. Lily's once enthusiastic letter to Santa filled with a wish list and promises of good behaviour, now sat unfinished in the drawer of her dressing table, abandoned midway through. She closed her eyes, longing for the enchanting dreams of Santa's world to visit her once more; she whispered a quiet wish into the stillness of the night. "Santa, are you real?" Overwhelmed by exhaustion and the weight of her swirling thoughts, Lily could no longer resist the call of sleep. She surrendered to its embrace, her eyelids gradually drooping until her emerald eyes gently closed, and she drifted into a peaceful slumber.

As Lily succumbed to the tender embrace of sleep, her reality gently dissolved, giving way to a dream of enchanting winter splendour. She found herself in a breathtaking wonderland, where each snowflake performed a delicate dance in the moon's silvery light. The air, crisp and invigorating, was filled with the harmonies of distant carollers, their voices blending in an ethereal chorus. Stepping forward, Lily left a trail of footprints in the untouched snow, her senses captivated by the mystical realm which had blossomed around her. Whispering snowflakes caressed her face, each one imparting tales of joy and marvel, while scents of pine and freshly baked cookies permeated the air.

Drawn by a radiant, golden light in the distance, Lily ventured forth with a heart brimming with curiosity. Her journey led her to a quaint cottage cradled between towering pines. Spirals of smoke rose from its chimney, and its windows sparkled with festive lights, casting a welcoming light. Approaching the cottage, Lily tapped lightly on the door, which swung open, revealing a room glowing with the gentle light of a fireplace. The interior exuded warmth and comfort; the fire's soft crackle, the ambient glow of candles, and the smell of cinnamon and spices enveloped her in a comforting embrace. She stepped inside; her gaze falling upon a bountiful feast laid out on a long wooden table. Roasted chestnuts, gingerbread, honey roasted hams and a large golden brown turkey, beckoned enticingly. Festive decorations adorned the room with garlands, wreaths, and tapestries depicting heartwarming Christmas scenes.

The room shimmered as the scene seamlessly transformed, as if carried by the magic of the dream. The cottage faded, and in its place, Lily found herself in a sleigh pulled by reindeer, gliding through the night sky. Beside her, Willow, once her pet dog, now a wise and talking companion, radiated an otherworldly glow. Willow's eyes sparkled with a profound connection to Lily. "Where are we headed?" Lily asked, her voice filled with wonder and glee.

"To places where the spirit of Christmas exists," Willow answered, the sound of Christmas bells echoing in the distance. "To realms where the spirit of the season lives in every snowflake and every star."

As they descended lower, the world below transformed into a lively mosaic of light and shadow. Villages twinkled below, windows aglow with hope and celebration. Below them, children wrapped in scarves and hats as they sculpted snowmen. Their laughter infusing the air with festive cheer. Lily watched a young girl, her hair as wild as the winter wind, struggling to place a top hat on her snowman. The sleigh landed in the soft snow.

"Let me help you," Lily offered, leaping from the sleigh, and striding through the snow.

With a tender touch, she fixed the hat on top of the snowman, which miraculously came to life, blinking its coal eyes and smiling in gratitude. The girl's laughter, pure and unrestrained, mingled with the distant melodies of Christmas carols.

"Thank you!" the girl exclaimed. "I'm Lucy. And you are?"

"I'm Lily," she responded, her heart brimming with an indescribable joy.

Together, they joined the other children, each snowman springing to life in a burst of magic, adding magic to the festivities. The snowmen's clumsy yet enthusiastic dance invited Lily to join in, and she did, dancing with them under the stars.

Eventually, Lily reluctantly said farewell to the children and returned to the sleigh. As they departed, the village remained aglow, its festive spirit pulsating with love and energy.

Their next destination was a serene forest, unlike any Lily had seen. Tall, majestic trees, cloaked in snow, created an atmosphere of tranquillity. "This was the Forest of Lost Toys," Willow explained, "A sanctuary for toys once cherished and then forgotten. Each toy held a story of love and laughter, now tinged with separation and sadness."

A worn teddy bear, one-eyed and tattered, caught Lily's attention. As she picked it up, it whispered a tale of once being a beloved companion to a little boy. Lily's heart ached for the bear and its companions, all once were central to a child's world, now residents of this heart breaking forest.

"We can't alter the past," Willow said, sensing Lily's emotions. "But we can create joy in the present. These toys can still bring happiness."

Motivated, Lily gathered the toys, promising them a future filled with love and laughter. The sleigh was soon brimming with toys, each radiating hope.

Departing the forest, Lily glanced back to see the trees shimmering in a silent farewell. The once cold and solemn haven now exuded warmth symbolising new beginnings.

Ascending into the night, the sky transformed into a canvas painted with the vibrant colours of the Northern Lights. Their journey reached its bittersweet end at a serene, snow-covered lake, where the moon's reflection danced upon the ice like a thousand tiny stars. As the sleigh slowed to a halt, Lily took a deep breath, feeling the chill of the night air seep into her bones. The sleigh was gently guided down until it landed amidst a gathering of wide-eyed, curious children. Their clothes were tattered and thin, hardly enough to protect them from the biting cold, but their faces were lit with the kind of wonder that only the truly innocent can possess. These were the forgotten souls, the little ones who had grown accustomed to empty bellies and cold nights, yet still found a way to dream. Lily's eyes welled with tears as they reached out with trembling hands, not for gifts or riches, but simply to touch the sleigh and believe, if only for a moment, that magic was real.

"Who are you?" asked a bright-eyed boy.

"I'm Lily, and this is Willow," she replied, her heart warmed by the surrounding joy.

"We're journeying to spread Christmas cheer," Willow added.

Lily told them to choose a toy from the sleigh. The children's faces lit up, each choosing a toy, their expressions breaking into smiles as they embraced their new friends. Watching the children, Lily's heart swelled with the simple joys of childhood and the enchantment of Christmas.

Overwhelmed with emotion, Lily turned to Willow. "Thank you for this incredible journey."

Willow nuzzled her affectionately. "Remember, Lily, Christmas isn't about grand gestures. It's about the small moments of joy and love."

With those parting words, Willow vanished, leaving Lily in the dawn's soft light. Lily opened her eyes and found herself back in her bedroom. She was astonished that morning had arrived so soon; her dream felt so real.

The next day, school was once again closed due to the snow and ice affecting the heating. Lily couldn't wait to see Sophie. She hurried through breakfast, barely tasting the toast her mother had buttered, and threw on her coat, determined to reach her best friend's house before the frost melted from the windows. When she finally found Sophie in their usual meeting spot by the old oak tree in the park, Lily's heart was pounding with excitement. "You won't believe it!" she exclaimed, eyes sparkling with wonder. "I had the most incredible dream last night. Willow, my old dog, came back to me in a dream; he took me on a sleigh ride. We flew across the stars! There were reindeer, and we landed by a lake where so many children were waiting… it was so real, Sophie, it was like magic!"

Sophie frowned and crossed her arms over her chest, her expression stern. "Lily, it was just a dream," she said, with that matter-of-fact tone she often used when she wanted to sound older than her years. "You know Santa isn't real, and neither is magic. I told you that yesterday."

"But it felt real," Lily insisted, her voice trembling as she recalled the warmth of Willow's paw in her hand, the sound of sleigh bells echoing in the night. "It was more than a dream, Sophie. I could feel the wind in my hair, and the snowflakes, they were cold on my cheeks! And the children… they were so happy, even though they had nothing." Lily's voice softened, her eyes drifting away as if seeing the scene unfold once more. "It was like Willow was trying to show me something, telling me Christmas is real."

Sophie sighed, rolling her eyes. "It was just your imagination." But as she turned to walk away, something in Lily's expression made her pause. "Why does it matter so much to you, anyway?" Sophie asked quietly, her voice softening just a little.

"Because... because maybe if we believe, even a little, it means we haven't lost something important," Lily whispered, clutching the locket around her neck that she had received last year for Christmas. She looked up, her eyes bright. "It means that maybe, just maybe, magic can still find us."

Sophie stared at her friend for a moment, the snow crunching beneath her boots as she shifted uncomfortably. "You're such a dreamer," she muttered, but there was a flicker of doubt in her eyes. "Maybe... maybe you should tell me more about Willow. What else did he say?"

A smile began to spread across Lily's face as she realised that, despite everything, maybe Sophie hadn't completely let go of her belief in Christmas. "Well, he told me that sometimes, the things we can't see are the most real of all," Lily began, and as she recounted every detail of her incredible journey, a faint glow of wonder flickered in Sophie's eyes.

"I don't care what you believe, I know Santa is real." Said Lily.

As the morning unfolded, Lily and Sophie wandered through the park, their breath visible in the crisp air, as if each exhale carried a piece of the magic Lily had spoken of. They trudged through the snow, kicking it off from under their boots sending tiny sprays of snow scattering into the air, glittering like diamonds. Lily's words flowed like a river, painting the dream so vividly that even Sophie couldn't help but get swept up in it. They found themselves at their favourite bench, an old wooden seat with peeling paint, overlooking a small frozen pond. It was their secret place, the one where they shared their hopes, fears, and dreams. Today, it felt different. Lily reached into her pocket and pulled out a tiny bell on a red ribbon. It jingled softly in the stillness of the morning air, and Sophie's eyes widened.

"Where did you get that?" Sophie asked.

"It was there on my windowsill when I woke up," Lily explained, her eyes shining with wonder. "It was from Willow's collar. I thought it was lost. I know it was. I think Willow wanted me to have something to remember, something to remind me that it wasn't just a dream."

Sophie gingerly reached out and touched the bell with the tip of her finger, half-expecting it to vanish. When it remained, solid and real, she felt a shiver run down her spine. They spent a couple of hours that day, sitting on the bench, talking about everything and nothing all at once. They shared stories of Christmases past, how Lily leaves cookies and carrots out every year, swearing she once heard sleigh bells in the middle of the night. For the first time in a long while, Sophie allowed herself to be swept up in the nostalgia, in the possibility that perhaps, there was more to the world than what she could see. The girls decided to head back to Lily's house, where the scent of cinnamon and pine filled the air. Lily's mother prepared hot chocolate for them, and the two girls sat by the crackling fireplace, warming their hands around the steaming mugs. The warmth seeped into their fingers, and it felt like the magic from Lily's dream was wrapping itself around them, pulling them closer.

Sophie glanced at the twinkling lights on the Christmas tree, her eyes reflecting the tiny stars of red, green, and gold. "Do you think Willow will come back?" she asked, her voice soft, almost fragile.

Lily nodded confidently. "I believe he will," she said. "I think he's always been there, waiting for us to notice him."

Sophie stared into the flames for a moment, her thoughts swirling like the embers dancing in the hearth. Then she looked at Lily, and a small smile tugged at the corners of her mouth. "You know, Lily," she said, "maybe Santa doesn't have to be real for Christmas to be magical. Maybe it's enough that we believe in each other."

Tears stung Lily's eyes, and she reached out to squeeze Sophie's hand. "That's the most magical thing of all," she whispered. They sat there, fingers entwined; two best friends who had found their way back to believing in something bigger than themselves. Snow began to fall softly outside, blanketing the world in a shimmering layer of Christmas magic.

That night, as Lily lay in bed, once again hoping for a dream as exciting as the one she experienced the night before. Lily was about to close her eyes when a soft, ethereal glow filled her room, casting an otherworldly luminescence upon the walls. Startled, she sat up and gasped, her heart beating rapidly.

A shimmering golden envelope appeared, as if out of thin air. It hovered in the air for a brief moment before gently descending onto her bed. Lily's eyes widened in astonishment, her breath caught in her throat. She reached out cautiously, her fingers trembling as she picked up the envelope.

The envelope was unlike anything she had ever seen before. Its paper felt metallic, and it was adorned with intricate designs of snowy landscapes and reindeer. The ink shimmered like the stars on a winter's night. With a mix of trepidation and curiosity, she gingerly opened it. She removed a beautifully crafted invitation.

"Lily," it began, the letters dancing in elegant calligraphy, "You're invited to the North Pole to meet Santa Claus and discover the magic of Christmas. Be in your room on the night of the 23rd, and all your questions will be answered.

P.S. you can bring a friend."

Astonishment washed over her, followed by a wave of curiosity and, perhaps, a glimmer of hope. Can this be real? Lily pondered, her doubts still lingering in the corners of her mind. What if this invitation held the answers she had been seeking all along? Lily knew she had to embark on this extraordinary journey to the North Pole. She clutched the invitation tightly to her chest, the mix of scepticism and wonder reflected in her eyes. Little did she realise her life was on the verge of transforming in unimaginable ways and the magic she questioned might be even more genuine than she had ever conceived. But how was she to get there? As the golden invitation rested in her trembling hands, Lily's mind raced with questions. Her heart whispered to her, urging her to embrace the possibility that magic still exists in her world.

"What do you think, Mr. Fluff?" she said softly, addressing her stuffed bear, who witnessed her doubts and now the strange occurrence in her room. Mr. Fluff sat on the nearby bedside table, his button eyes seemingly alive with curiosity.

Lily realised she had no choice but to accept the invitation, with Mr. Fluff as her silent witness to this strange event. The glow of the room seemed to beckon her toward an adventure she had only dreamed of before. Gathering her courage, she made her decision.

"I'm going," Lily declared to Mr. Fluff, her voice filled with both trepidation and excitement. She carefully replaced the invitation in the envelope and placed it in her drawer next to the unfinished letter to Santa for safekeeping. As she settled back under her covers, the room gradually returned to its normal state, the soft glow fading away. Lily's thoughts raced as she thought of the journey ahead. She pondered what she would say to Santa if she really met him. The questions which had plagued her for the last couple of days now seemed trivial in the face of this unexpected opportunity.

The next morning, Lily burst into the kitchen, her cheeks flushed with excitement, waving the envelope in her hand. "Mum! Look what I've got!"

Her mother, rolling out cookies at the counter, turned with a smile. "What is it, darling?"

"It's an invitation!" Lily's voice quivered with barely contained joy. "To visit Santa! At the North Pole!"

"Really?" Her mother wiped her hands on her apron, curiosity sparkling in her eyes. "That sounds magical. Tell me more."

Lily bounced on her toes, her words tumbling out in a rush. "It says I can bring a friend. Oh, Mum, can I? Please, can I go?"

"Let me see it... where did this come from?"

Lily handed over the envelope, "It just appeared, last night. I was lying in bed and it just appeared in a glowing light. I knew Santa was real!" She exclaimed.

"Are you sure it just... appeared?"

"I promise mum, it was just like magic."

Her mum pondered the situation for a few minutes, 'it certainly feels special.' She thought. The invitation glowed in her hands and sent a shimmer of magic through her fingers. Her mother's smile widened. "Of course, not everyone gets an offer like this. Who do you want to take?"

Lily's brow furrowed in thought. "Sophie! Maybe I can get her to believe in Christmas and Santa again."

"That's a wonderful idea." Her mother nodded approvingly. "Santa's workshop, wow I bet it's a sight to see."

Lily's eyes shone. "Do you think we'll see elves? And the reindeer?"

"I'm sure you will." Her mother chuckled.

"Really?" Lily's voice rose in awe.

"Just remember, it's a special place. You must be on your best behaviour." she said with a loving smile.

Lily nodded vigorously. "I will Mum. I promise!"

Her mother pulled her into a warm hug. "I know you will, darling. This is going to be an adventure you'll remember forever."

Lily hugged her back, her heart swelling with excitement. "Thank you, Mum. This is the best Christmas ever!"

"How are you going to get there?"

"I don't know? It says we have to be in my bedroom on the night of the 23rd."

"Then you will have to do just that. We will have to see what we can do to rekindle Sophie's belief in Santa. I'm sure she will enjoy the experience more as a believer."

Later that morning whilst on her way to school, Lily practically floated on air, her heart fluttering with anticipation. She was unable to contain her excitement to share the incredible magic of the golden invitation with Sophie, her unwavering best friend, who had been her confidante through every adventure, big or small.

During playtime, Lily spotted Sophie sitting on a swing, lost in thought as she pushed herself gently back and forth. Lily approached her, the precious invitation clutched in her hand like a treasured secret.

"Sophie!" she called out with enthusiasm, her voice carrying the excitement bubbling within her.

Sophie looked up, her eyes meeting Lily's with a mixture of curiosity and affection. "Hey, Lily," she greeted her friend with a warm smile, "what's got you so excited today?"

Lily took a deep breath, her heart pounding with anticipation. She decided to share her newfound discovery, no matter how unbelievable it might seem. "You won't believe what happened last night," she began, her voice a hushed whisper filled with wonder.

"You had another magical dream about Santa?" A hint of sarcasm in her tone.

"No, I received an invitation, Sophie. An invitation to meet Santa Claus at the North Pole!"

Sophie's eyes widened in surprise, and she hopped off the swing to join Lily. "Santa Claus? Are you serious, Lily?"

Lily nodded passionately, her red hair bouncing with excitement. "I couldn't believe it myself, but it's real! The invitation appeared in my room, and it was filled with magic. It says I can go to the North Pole and meet Santa to discover the true magic of Christmas!"

Sophie's brows furrowed, her scepticism evident. "Lily, are you sure about this? It sounds so... unbelievable."

Lily understood her friend's hesitation. After all, she had been grappling with doubts about Santa herself. "I know it's hard to believe, but it happened. And we're going," she declared with newfound determination.

"We're going? And how are we supposed to get to the North Pole? Get real Lily."

"Look, here's the invitation." She said, holding up the golden envelope. "It says we must be in my room on the night of the 23rd. You could tell your mum we are having a sleepover at mine before Christmas."

Sophie gave an unbelieving smile. "Are you sure this is not from Willy Wonka?" she scoffed, examining the golden envelope.

"It's real, I tell you. I would never tell my best friend a lie," she insisted.

Sophie studied Lily's earnest expression, her doubts giving way to curiosity as she examined the envelope again and then its contents. "If it's real," she said cautiously, "It could be an incredible adventure."

Lily's eyes sparkled with gratitude as she embraced her friend. "Thank you for understanding, Sophie. I couldn't do this without you."

Sophie returned the hug warmly. "Of course, Lily. Friends stick together through thick and thin." She said, her disbelief remaining at the forefront of her mind.

Lily nodded, her heart warmed by the unwavering support of her best friend. "I promise, Sophie, it's real." Her eyes were alive with excitement.

That night Lily was in her bedroom her excitement continued to build, and she meticulously prepared for her journey to the North Pole. She packed her warmest clothes, her trusty notebook, and a pen to document her extraordinary adventure.

Outside, the world was blanketed in snow, a serene white canvas that seemed to echo her own anticipation. The soft glow of the moonlight filtered through her window, casting a dreamlike quality over her room. She peered outside, watching the snowflakes gently descend, each one unique, just like the incredible journey that awaited her. Her excitement was evident, yet a part of her mind grappled with the reality of it all. Meeting Santa Claus was a childhood dream, one which seemed too fantastical to be true. But the magic in her heart, fuelled by the enchanted invitation, whispered promises of a reality beyond her wildest dreams.

The house was quiet. Lily climbed into bed, snuggling under her cosy blankets. Her thoughts wandered to Sophie, wondering if she too was lying awake, pondering their impending adventure. She closed her eyes, trying to will herself to sleep. Images of the North Pole danced in her mind, a land of endless snow, magical elves, and the jolly, red-suited Santa Claus. She imagined them exploring this wonderland, their laughter echoing amidst the snow-capped trees and sparkling icicles. As sleep finally began to claim her, Lily felt a sense of peace. With these thoughts warming her heart, Lily drifted into a deep, restful sleep, her dreams filled with visions of the magical journey ahead. The snow outside continued to fall, blanketing the world in its serene, white embrace, as if mother nature herself was preparing Lily for her magical journey to the North Pole.

Chapter 2

It was the afternoon of the 14th of December. Sophie sat at home, gazing out of the window at the swirling snowflakes, her heart heavy with a sense of loss. Where there was once a bright, glittering joy in her spirit for Christmas, now there lingered only a faint echo, a dull ache of what used to be. This last year had changed everything for her. In a quiet moment, her mum revealed the truth about Santa Claus. She did it gently but firmly. This lifted the magic veil that covered Christmas. Sophie's belief in the Christmas wonders started to dissolve. It was like snow melting in the sun's warmth. But hope, as it often does, lived in the form of her best friend, Lily. A believer with a heart as warm as a Yule Log fire.

Lily was determined to reignite the extinguished flame of Christmas spirit in Sophie's heart. Today, they were embarking on a journey to a place known as the 'Christmas Village', a seasonal spectacle of wonder and fun. The morning air was crisp. The sky was a painted canvas of pastel hues. Lily bounded up to Sophie's front door with excitement. Her eyes sparkled with anticipation. "Sophie, today's the day! The day we discover the true magic of Christmas," Lily exclaimed, her words a melody of joy and conviction. Sophie offered a small smile, her scepticism still a heavy cloak around her shoulders. "Lily, you know I don't believe in... all that, not anymore."

Lily took Sophie's hands in hers. "Just trust me, okay? We'll have a great time." Before Sophie could protest, Lily's parents called them over, ready to depart. The journey to the Christmas Village was filled with chatter about elves, reindeer, and the countless wonders they were about to witness. Sophie listened, her doubts a whisper among Lily's tales of magic. When they arrived, the girls were welcomed by a sight even more spectacular than they expected. Little did they know the Christmas Village harboured secrets beyond the festive facade. Magic swirled in the air, a kind not written about in storybooks but felt deep within the soul. This was a magic born out of belief, of hope, and of the pure, unadulterated joy which

Christmas brings. The adventure which awaited them in the Christmas Village was more than a journey through a winter wonderland. It would be a journey to the very essence of Christmas.

Lily and Sophie giggled with excitement as they stepped out of the car and into the dazzling Christmas' Village. The air was filled with the sweet scent of freshly baked gingerbread and the soft glow of fairy lights adorned every building.

"You two go and enjoy yourselves. We will meet up in the cafeteria in 3 hours' time," said Lily's mum, "And be careful!" She shouted after them.

The two friends held hands and skipped towards a large ice-skating rink. In the heart of the quaint village, the outdoor Christmas ice skating rink transformed into a picturesque winter wonderland. Twinkling lights danced and festive decorations adorned the barriers casting a magical glow upon the ice. Laughter and music filled the air as skaters glided gracefully across the ice, their cheeks rosy with cold and excitement. The rink itself glistened like a giant mirror. At its centre stood a beautifully decorated Christmas tree, protected by a metal barrier. The tree, adorned with colourful ornaments appearing to stretch upward to touch the sky, and topped with a brilliant star.

Lily's eyes sparkled with delight as they approached the rink, her gaze drawn to the majestic Christmas tree at its centre. Its ornaments shimmered like jewels under the twinkling lights. "Sophie, this is going to be so much fun!" she exclaimed, her voice echoing her excitement.

Sophie's laughter rang out, full of joy. "It's beautiful, Lily! I can't wait to skate around the tree."

They each hired a pair of skates and swiftly laced them up, their fingers working deftly, each loop and knot heightening their anticipation. Stepping onto the ice, a moment of unsteadiness struck them, but holding hands, they found their balance. Gradually, their movements smoothed out as they adapted to the slippery ice under their skates.

The air was alive with music, a mixture of classic carols and cheerful festive tunes infusing the atmosphere with merriment. Lily and Sophie moved rhythmically to the music, their laughter blending seamlessly with the ambient sounds of the rink.

"We're like professional ice skaters!" Sophie exclaimed, her voice bright with exhilaration and a touch of sarcasm.

Lily twirled, feeling the bite of the cold air on her cheeks, which flushed a playful pink. "This is the most fun I've had in ages," she replied, her eyes alight with joy.

People moved gracefully on the ice, filling the rink with activity and creating a beautiful winter scene full of joy. Other skaters gliding in seamless harmony, their figures casting long, playful shadows under the myriad of lights. These shadows danced on the ice, creating an enchanting spectacle. Children, bundled in colourful winter clothes, darted about with playful energy, their laughter mingling with the crisp air. Couples skated in tender unison, each pair a closed circle of affection, lost in their own little worlds.

As Lily and her friend neared the Christmas tree, its twinkling lights cast a warm, golden glow over the rink. The tree stood majestic and tall, its branches laden with ornaments which shimmered and sparkled, reflecting the joy of the season. Atop the tree, a magnificent star shone brightly, a beacon of Christmas spirit, its light reaching the farthest corners of the rink and touching everyone with its magic.

People, wrapped up in warm scarves and mittens, packed the area surrounding the rink. Their faces aglow with joy, and reflecting the colourful lights. Skaters of all ages shared the ice, from toddlers tentatively hanging onto penguin skate aids to teenagers performing elegant pirouettes, their graceful movements a testament to hours of practice.

Christmas carols, brimming with joy, floated through the air, the melodies blending harmoniously with the delightful aromas filling the rink. The scents of gingerbread and roasted chestnuts emanated from charming red carts adorned with elegant gold script. These carts enhanced the festive atmosphere, positioned as they were along the bustling streets. The merry tunes and enticing smells beckoned passers-by, inviting them to partake in all of the season's delights and traditions. They left the ice rink and returned their skates, the cold air nipping at their faces. Sophie squeezed Lily's hand. "This place is amazing! Let's get some gingerbread."

Lily turned to Sophie, her eyes brimming with the uncontainable wonder. "I wonder if the North Pole looks just like this?" she queried, her voice imbued with curiosity.

Sophie, with a gentle smile playing on her lips, looked at her friend. Her response carried the soothing tone of a seasoned storyteller, not wanting to crush Lily's dream. "Perhaps, Lily," she replied. "Perhaps."

They laughed as they continued their journey through the village. A place where the magic of Christmas was as tangible as the icy chill in the air and the comforting warmth of their friendship.

As they continued exploring, they stumbled upon a quaint toy shop with a sign which read "Mrs Christmas's Toy Emporium." The doorbell bounced and jingled as they entered, and a kindly old lady with rosy cheeks greeted them. "Welcome, dear children! I'm Mrs Christmas," she said with a warm smile. Lily and Sophie exchanged glances, captivated by the twinkling lights and shelves filled with toys. "Please, have a good look around. I'll be over here if you need any help." Said the old lady.

As they ventured further into Mrs Christmas's Toy Emporium, Lily and Sophie found themselves in a world of wonder. The air was perfumed with a sweet scent of gingerbread and cinnamon, and the soft, magical glow of fairy lights bathed every corner, casting playful shadows. The shelves, carved in intricate patterns, were laden with an array of toys that seemed to come from every era and every corner of the world. There were handcrafted wooden soldiers standing proudly next to gleaming model trains chugging along miniature tracks. Dolls with porcelain faces and silk dresses sat elegantly beside puzzles sparkling with intrigue and promise.

Sophie's eyes widened as she spotted a vintage carousel, its horses painted in bright colours, their manes flowing as if caught in a gentle breeze. "Look at this, Lily!" she exclaimed, her voice filled with awe. "It's like something out of a dream."

Lily, meanwhile, was drawn to a shelf holding a collection of crystal balls and snow globes. Each one shimmered with a light of its own, and inside, tiny scenes played out, one a snow-covered village, and another a starry night sky, but one, in particular, caught her eye, a Christmas scene of ice skaters on a frozen lake.

"Mrs Christmas," Lily called out. "How much are these? They're like little worlds of their own."

Mrs Christmas, who had been arranging a display of teddy bears, looked up and walked over, a twinkle in her eye. "Ah, my dear, these are very special," she said, picking up a snow globe.

Lily's eyes were still drawn to the intricate snow globe which looked just like the Christmas village. She reached out to pick it up.

Mrs Christmas noticed her interest. "Ah, that's a special one, dear. It's said to hold a bit of Christmas magic."

Sophie raised an eyebrow. "Christmas magic? What does it do?"

Mrs Christmas chuckled softly. "Well, it's said that if you make a wish while holding the snow globe, the magic within might just make your wish come true."

Lily looked at Sophie, a glimmer of hope in her eyes. "Do you think it's true, Sophie?"

Sophie shrugged, a mischievous grin on her face. "There's only one way to find out, Lily. Make a wish."

Lily gave the snow globe a shake, held the snow globe close to her heart, and closed her eyes. She whispered her wish, a wish for the joy and magic of Christmas, to return to Sophie's heart. The snow globe began to shimmer and glow, as the tiny snowflakes swirled inside it, dancing to an unseen melody. Lily gasped, her heart racing as she experienced a surge of warmth and happiness washing over her.

Sophie's eyes widened in amazement. "Lily, look!"

They watched in awe as the snow globe transformed into Santa's Grotto. Mrs Christmas clapped her hands with delight. "It's the Christmas magic, my dears! That's the magic of believing!"

Lily and Sophie laughed and Sophie sensed her doubts lift a little.

"How much is it?" Lily asked, still clutching the globe.

"For you, dear, ten pounds."

Lily paid the ten pounds, and Mrs Christmas packed it safely in a cardboard box.

"Where shall we go next?" asked Lily.

The Christmas Village was alive with festive cheer as Lily and Sophie strolled through the cobblestone streets. The air was filled with the smells of Christmas, and the soft glow of twinkling lights enveloping the village in a warm embrace.

Lily's eyes sparkled with excitement. "Sophie, I can't believe how magical this place is. It's like stepping into a Christmas fairy tale, isn't it?"

Sophie grinned; her cheeks rosy from the cold.

"Do you still believe there is no Santa?" Lily's voice was soft and gentle.

"Yes, Although I do enjoy the magic of this place. I still can't see my mum lying to me. Why would she?"

Lily paused for a second, "It could be due to the fact she has stopped believing herself."

Sophie shrugged as they kept walking. As they wandered further around the village, they came across a small, forested area on the outskirts. Tall evergreen trees stood proudly; their branches heavy with fresh snow. It was at that location Lily and Sophie perceived a soft, mournful sound, similar to a gentle whimper of an animal.

Lily frowned and strained her ears to listen again. "Did you hear that, Sophie?"

Sophie nodded; her curiosity piqued. "I think so. Let's follow the sound."

They ventured further into the woods, guided by the mysterious sound. It led them to a clearing, where they discovered a young reindeer with large, soulful eyes. It was clear the reindeer was lost and in distress.

Lily's heart went out to the creature. "Oh, poor thing. It must have strayed from Santa's reindeer enclosure in the village."

Sophie approached the reindeer slowly, extending her hand with caution. "It's okay, little one. We won't hurt you."

The reindeer, seemingly reassured by Sophie's gentle demeanour, took a tentative step forward. It nuzzled Sophie's hand, as though seeking comfort. Sophie sensed a warm sensation pass through her body, and an unusual connection to the reindeer.

Lily watched in awe. "Sophie, it's like the reindeer trusts you."

Sophie smiled; her eyes filled with wonder. "I think it does. Let's try to help it get back."

Lily and Sophie decided to lead the lost reindeer out of the woods and back into the heart of the Christmas Village. Sophie took hold of the reindeer's halter and they slowly walked back to the village. As they did, people gathered around, amazed by the sight of the two young girls with the reindeer. Lily's parents spotted them and approached, their faces a mix of surprise and wonder. Lily's mother spoke softly, "Lily, Sophie, what are you doing with one of Santa's reindeer?"

"We found it by those trees. It appeared to be crying and lost. We have brought it back to the village."

A choir began to sing Christmas carols, creating a festive atmosphere which washed over them all. The little reindeer seemed to respond to the music, its once-worried expression transforming into one of delight.

Sophie leaned close to Lily and whispered, "Hey Lily, it's like the reindeer is listening to the Christmas songs!"

Lily nodded, her eyes shining with understanding. "It's like magic."

The man who looked after the reindeer appeared from around the corner. "Ah, there you are," he said to the reindeer. "Where did you find Frosty?"

"Over by the trees." Sophie replied.

"He is always escaping." Laughed the man. "Thank you for bringing him back. He took hold of the halter from Sophie and led it away back to the reindeer paddock.

As night time approached, the sky grew darker. The stars twinkled brightly in the fresh night air. The coloured fairy lights illuminated the village, creating a truly enchanting atmosphere. The bright colours of red, green, and gold lit up the snowy cottages and paths, making the village look like a scene from a Christmas storybook. The flickering lights danced happily, creating a magical atmosphere in the village which made all worries disappear.

Accompanied by her parents, Lily, along with her friend Sophie, ventured into the cosy warmth of the cafeteria for afternoon tea. Following their delightful break, the two girls, with renewed energy, set out once again to discover the remaining wonders of the village.

"Be back in one hour. It's nearly time to head off home." Lily's mum stressed.

Lily turned to her mum, "We will!" she shouted, as she skipped away, holding Sophie's hand. Wrapped cosily in their winter clothing, they set out to explore the village once more. It looked even more magical now in the early evening twilight.

"Sophie, look!" Exclaimed Lily as she pointed towards Santa's grotto. "Did you see them?"

Sophie looked to where Lily was pointing. "What am I looking at?"

"Didn't you see the elves?"

Sophie pressed her lips together and gave a slight shake of her head, "No, what elves?"

"The elves went into Santa's grotto, they moved so fast. Let's go check it out."

"They probably work there Lily. They're not going to be real elves." Sophie replied, her voice tinged with sarcasm. "But... okay, let's check it out."

The girls hurried towards Santa's Grotto, the path lit by strands of twinkling fairy lights. As they approached, the sound of laughter and Christmas music filled their ears.

Lily tugged at Sophie's sleeve, her eyes wide with excitement. "There! look! Did you see them this time?" she whispered.

Sophie squinted, trying to catch a glimpse of whatever Lily had seen. "Maybe... but they could just be people dressed as elves, you know."

Undeterred, Lily pulled her friend closer to the entrance of the grotto. "Let's go inside."

The interior was a wonderland of Christmas magic, with sparkling decorations, an enormous Christmas tree, and a cosy fireplace. The air was filled with the scent of pine and chocolate, the sound of soft jingle bells echoing around the grotto.

"Welcome to Santa's Grotto!" a deep voice boomed. A man dressed as Santa sat in a large, ornate chair, his eyes twinkling behind round, gold-rimmed spectacles. Children were lined up, waiting for their turn to speak with him. Lily took out her mobile phone and took a couple of photos of Santa. She lined Sophie up and then took a selfie of them both with Santa in the background.

Finally, Santa beckoned them forward with a warm smile. "Ho! ho! ho! And what would you two like for Christmas?"

"It's okay Santa, my mum has Christmas covered." Sophie replied.

Lily stepped forward, her eyes shining. "Santa, we saw your elves outside. They were real, weren't they?"

Santa's smile widened, and he let out a hearty chuckle. "Well, my elves are quite busy this time of year. It's possible you saw them."

"Can you prove you are the real Santa?" asked Sophie, her eyes wide with curiosity and a hint of scepticism.

"You want a little proof?" Santa continued, still smiling broadly as he reached into his pocket, "I have something for you." He handed each girl a small silver bell. "These are special. They'll only ring for those who truly believe." Santa nodded sagely, "Belief in the magic of Christmas isn't about just seeing, it's about feeling it in your heart. The warmth of a family, the joy of giving, the happiness of being together, that's where the real magic lies."

"But how do we really know it's all true?" Sophie persisted, turning the bell over in her hand. "And what if we can't hear the bell?"

Santa smiled gently. "Just give it time. Sometimes belief grows stronger as you grow." Then with a small sigh he uttered, "But, as some people grow, their belief lessens... Anyway, Christmas is a time for magic. Keep that bell close and one day, you might just hear it ring. Remember, open your heart to the magic of Christmas."

Lily gave her bell a little shake, they heard a faint but definite jingle. Sophie gave hers a shake... nothing, not a sound. Sophie looked disappointed.

"Here, swap." said Lily,

Sophie gave Lily's bell a shake. Again, not a sound. Lily gave Sophie's bell a shake, and there it was... a faint jingle.

Santa looked at Sophie's disappointed face, "Remember, you have to truly believe, then you will hear it ring, I promise."

The girls thanked Santa and stepped outside. With the bells in their hands, they gave them a tentative shake, still no sound came from Sophie's bell.

Lily, her eyes brimming with hope, turned to Sophie and said in an encouraging tone, "Perhaps all you need to do is to believe a little more."

Sophie shrugged, her usual scepticism waning in the face of the evening's wonders. "Yeah, possibly."

As they wandered through the village, the twinkling lights and the shimmering full moon draped everything around them in an enchanting glow. Lost in conversation, they talked about their Christmas wishes and wondered if the golden invitation was real. Was it possible the magic promised would truly unfold on the 23rd?

Suddenly, Lily stopped. "Do you hear that?"

Sophie listened. In the distance, a faint sound of sleigh bells jingled through the air. The sound of the bells grew louder; the girls scanned the night sky.

"I can hear the bells, but I can't see anything," said Sophie, sounding a little disappointed.

They stood looking skywards as the sound of the bells grew faint and finally disappeared. Flakes of snow began to gently fall, each flake sparkling under the moonlight like tiny stars drifting down to earth. They twirled and danced around the girls, landing on their faces and eyelashes.

Lily's eyes sparkled with the reflected light of the snowflakes. "Maybe," she whispered, "the magic is starting already. Is it possible it's not just about seeing Santa or the sleigh but believing in him before we can actually see him."

Sophie felt a smile tug at the corners of her mouth, her heart-warming despite the cold. The uncertainty which usually clung to her thoughts began to melt away a little, like the snow on their mittens.

As they neared the end of the village, a chorus of carollers greeted them, their voices rising and falling in harmonious melodies. The girls paused to listen, their faces aglow with the nearby streetlamp's golden light. It felt as if the entire world was holding its breath, waiting for magic to unfold.

"Let's make a pact," Lily suddenly declared, her voice steadier than before. "Let's keep these bells safe," she said, a new resolve in her voice. "And let's keep believing, at least till the 23rd. Who knows what might happen?" With a renewed sense of wonder, the girls tucked the bells into their pockets and continued their walk. Sophie nodded, her eyes shining. "I promise," she said, and the two girls happily headed home through the snow, their minds filled with thoughts of the mysterious 23rd and the magic that awaited them.

The night sky was a canvas of twinkling lights, but one star shone brighter than the rest. Lily, her eyes wide with wonder, pointed upwards. "Look, Sophie! That's a wishing star. It's special. It listens to your heart's deepest wishes."

Sophie, a glimmer of curiosity in her eyes, gazed at the star. "Really? Does it really grant wishes?" she asked, her scepticism softened by the magical atmosphere.

Lily nodded eagerly. "Yes! Let's make a wish. But remember, it has to be a secret."

The girls closed their eyes, each whispering their wish to the star. Sophie's heart fluttered with a hope she hadn't felt in years. Maybe, just maybe, the star could rekindle her belief in the magic of Christmas. As they opened their eyes, the star seemed to twinkle even brighter, as if acknowledging their wishes. The snow continued to fall softly around them. Each step they took seeming lighter than the last, as if they were walking on the cusp of something miraculous.

Chapter 3

As the night wrapped the world outside in darkness, Sophie nestled under her blankets, her mind filled with a blend of childhood memories and hopeful dreams. Her room was peaceful, softly lit by moonbeams sneaking through the curtains. In these tranquil moments, a delicate ringing broke the stillness. It was faint and whimsical, reminiscent of the chimes one might hear in a dreamy, faraway land.

The mysterious sound appeared to originate from the quaint, ornate bell which dangled elegantly from her dressing-table mirror, a special gift she had received from the smiling Santa in the Christmas village, where he had given one each to her and Lily. Intrigued and slightly puzzled, Sophie stretched out to turn on her night-light, which bathed the room in a warm, amber glow.

There, in the gentle light, the bell appeared to sway ever so slightly, as if moved by an unseen hand. Sophie's eyes narrowed in concentration, discerning if what she was seeing was real or just her imagination playing tricks. She held her breath, listening intently, but as suddenly as it had appeared, the sound vanished, leaving behind a profound silence.

Shaking her head, Sophie attributed the sound to her imagination, a trick of her sleepy mind. She turned off the night-light, surrendering to the embrace of sleep, her thoughts dissolving into the peaceful oblivion of her dreams.

The next morning, as the first rays of sunlight crept through her window, casting patterns on the walls, Sophie's eyes fluttered open. A sense of curiosity still lingered from the previous night's mystery. As she sat up, stretching her arms wide and yawning, her gaze fell upon her dressing table. There, amidst her usual array of trinkets and treasures, lay an unfamiliar package, it was neatly wrapped and patiently awaiting discovery.

Sophie's heart skipped a beat. She slipped out of bed, her bare feet touching the soft carpet as she approached the dressing table. Her hands, trembling with a mix of excitement and disbelief, as she reached out for the package. The wrapping paper was delicate, adorned with intricate patterns of snowflakes and reindeer in a winter scene, as if it had been wrapped in the very essence of Christmas itself.

Carefully, she unwrapped the package, revealing its contents. Inside lay a plush reindeer, its fur worn by the passage of time. One of its eyes was still intact, and sparkled with an enigmatic twinkle, reminiscent of the star they had wished upon the previous night. The other eye was missing, lending the toy an air of endearing imperfection.

A floodgate of memories opened in Sophie's mind. This wasn't just any toy; it was the very reindeer she had received from Santa, years before during a previous childhood visit to the Christmas village. She remembered clutching it tightly as she fell asleep on Christmas Eve, the joy and wonder of the season alive in her young heart.

But how had this toy, long lost, found its way back to her now, after so many years? The mystery expanded, blossoming into something similar to a magical tale or an incredibly vivid dream. It felt thrillingly real, as if it had leaped straight out of a fairy tale. This was more than a mere coincidence; it felt like a sign, a message from the past, reminding her of the joy and innocence she once knew. Sophie held the reindeer close, its one-eyed gaze seeming to peer into her soul, reawakening feelings of wonder and belief she thought she had lost.

Sophie raced down to show it to her mum. "Did you put this reindeer in my room last night?" Sophie asked, holding up the small toy with a curious glint in her eye.

"No, darling. Where did it come from?" her mum replied, genuinely puzzled but noticing the familiar toy. "Isn't this the little reindeer you were so attached to when you were younger? The one you were so upset about losing when you were six?"

"Mum, do you remember when I lost it? We looked everywhere for it!" Sophie's voice filled with astonishment and a growing excitement.

"Yes, love, we turned the house upside down looking for it. You were so heartbroken," her mum recalled, a hint of nostalgia in her tone. "But how on earth did it find its way back to you after all these years?"

"I don't know mum. It was on my dressing table. It was wrapped in this." She said, producing the wrapping paper.

Sophie's mum looked confused. "Where on earth could it have come from? I certainly did not put it there."

Sophie shrugged, her mind racing with possibilities. "I don't know, but it feels like... like maybe it's a sign this Christmas is going to be really special this year."

Her mum smiled, confusion creeping into her mind by her daughter's renewed sense of wonder. "Well, maybe it is, sweetheart. Maybe it is."

That morning, Sophie rushed to school to show Lily the mysterious gift. "Look, Lily! This is the toy I got when I was little, after visiting Santa. I lost it years ago, and now it's back."

Lily's eyes widened in amazement. "See, it's the magic of Christmas."

"The star, the wishing star. I wished for proof that Santa was real. The star... I think it listened!"

"Wow, Sophie! That's incredible! The star really did grant your wish. Where did you find it?"

"It was wrapped in Christmas paper and left on my dressing table. I asked my mum if she had found it and left it there. She said it wasn't her. Do you think it really was the star? Did your wish come true?" Sophie asked eagerly.

"I'm not sure." said Lily. "It may take a while before I find out if my wish comes true."

The school's heating was repaired, and it was now in the midst of a festive initiative, seeking enthusiastic volunteers to bring the joy of Christmas to the village. Among those who stepped forward were Lily and Sophie, eager to contribute. They had volunteered for a particularly heartwarming task, to assist the village's Santa in delivering gifts to the residents of the nearby elderly care home. This activity was scheduled for this Saturday, and both girls were filled with excitement and anticipation.

As the weekend arrived, the girls, dressed in festive attire, made their way to the meeting point outside the residential home. The air was crisp, and the village streets were sparsely decorated with lights and festive decorations. The sound of a deep, cheerful voice soon greeted them.

"Hello, young ladies," boomed Santa, his voice as jolly as the bells which jingled with his every movement. He stood there in his bright red suit, his eyes twinkling with merriment behind his fake round spectacles. "Are you two my helpers today?" he asked, a warm smile spreading across his bearded face.

The girls nodded eagerly. "Yes, Santa. We're here to help deliver the presents," Lily replied, her voice filled with excitement.

Santa's laugh, hearty and infectious, filled the air. "Wonderful! We have many gifts to deliver and many smiles to bring."

"What do you need us to do?" asked Sophie.

"Well, we need to hand out these gifts, but more importantly, we need to talk and listen to these folk. They have lived many years and have a vast array of stories to tell."

"Why is that important?" Sophie asked curiously.

"Many of them no longer have family or friends to visit them. Many of them feel lonely, especially at this time of year. So, we need to make them feel loved and feel they are not alone, that people do care about them."

This pulled at their delicate young heart-strings. "We will talk to them, and listen to them," promised Sophie.

All the residents of the care home were gathered in the lounge area. The large room was transformed into a warm, welcoming haven of Christmas cheer. As they entered the room, the comforting scent of pine immediately greeted their senses from the grand Christmas tree which stood majestically in one corner. The tree, almost reaching the ceiling, was adorned with an array of colourful lights which were twinkling merrily. Shimmering tinsel and handmade ornaments graced the tree, each piece carrying its own story from each of the residents.

Garlands laced with holly, berries, and even more twinkling fairy lights were strung gracefully along the walls, intertwining with wreaths featuring bows of deep red and gold. The windows were decorated with delicate snowflake decals and cheerful scenes of winter wonderlands, offering views of the gently falling snow outside.

Comfortable armchairs and sofas were arranged in cosy clusters around the room, inviting residents and visitors alike to sit and enjoy each other's company. Each seating area was accented with plush red and green pillows, and in the centre, a large, ornate rug provided a soft texture underfoot.

Nearby, a fireplace crackled with a roaring fire, the mantel above it festooned with garlands and Christmas candles. The hearth became a popular gathering spot, where the residents could bask in the warmth of the fire and share stories of Christmases past.

On one side of the room, a piano sat decked with festive decor. Here, residents and guests often gathered for a sing-along of classic Christmas carols, filling the room with the joyful sounds of the season. Next to the piano, a table was laden with an array of Christmas treats, gingerbread cookies, fruitcake, and hot chocolate, all lovingly prepared by the staff and some of the residents who loved to bake.

The lounge area was filled with activities all day, with residents engaging in Christmas crafts and decorating, and local school children visiting and performing festive songs and dances. It was a place where memories were shared and new ones made. Where the spirit of the season touched every heart, bringing smiles to faces and warmth to souls. In the evenings, the room took on a magical quality. As the lights dimmed slightly, the Christmas tree glowed more brightly, casting a serene ambiance to the room. Residents often sat quietly in this tranquil setting, some reminiscing, some simply enjoying the peace and beauty of the moment.

This area, at Christmas time, became more than just a part of the care home; it was a symbol of community, love, and the timeless spirit of the season.

Santa let out a booming, "Ho! Ho! Ho! Merry Christmas!" as he entered the room, walking behind the girls.

"Seeing as you are all on the 'Nice List', I have brought presents for you all, Ho! Ho! Ho!"

Santa handed Lily a present to give to one of the elderly lady's, while Sophie handed a large gift wrapped in purple Christmas paper to one of the old ladies. "Thank you very much." She said with such gratitude.

"You're welcome." Sophie replied.

The old lady smiled and beckoned Sophie to sit in an empty chair next to hers. "Are you looking forward to Santa paying you a visit?"

"I don't really believe in Santa. My mum said he wasn't real."

The old lady paused; her eyes met the floor. She took a deep breath and replied, "When I was a girl, during the war, I went to live with a woman in the countryside. We had to be evacuated, you see, because of the bombing; it was safer than living in the towns. The woman who was looking after me, Mrs Thompson, she told me Santa wasn't real. I remember feeling sad for a long time. Then, one snowy night close to Christmas, I was wrapped up in bed. The world outside was blanketed in snow, and everything was so quiet, so still. I remember lying in bed watching the snow gently falling, the sadness heavy in my heart. I was missing my home and my parents. Anyway, I must have dozed off, because when I woke, at the foot of my bed lay a beautiful, handcrafted doll. It was unlike anything I'd ever seen, with golden curls and eyes which seemed to sparkle in the moonlight."

Sophie's eyes sparkled with intrigue. "A doll? Just appeared at the foot of your bed?"

The old lady nodded, "It was like magic."

"That sounds a bit like what happened to me."

"You got a doll too?"

"No, it was a reindeer I lost when I was little; it mysteriously appeared the other day. Someone had wrapped it and left it on my dressing table. No one knows where it came from."

The old lady merely smiled and continued with her story. "Mrs Thompson was flustered, too. She didn't know where it came from, either. She accused me of stealing it, saying I must have taken it from one of the local shops. But I hadn't. I didn't even know it existed until that moment."

"What happened next?" Sophie asked, leaning forward.

"The next day, Mrs Thompson took me to every shop in the village, asking if they'd lost a doll. But none of them had. They all said they didn't stock anything like it. The police were even called, but no one had reported a doll missing."

Sophie frowned. "She called the police on you? That must have been scary."

"It was," the old lady agreed. "But then, something wonderful happened.

The policeman, a kind man with a gentle smile, after inspecting the doll, knelt down to my level, "This is a unique doll," he said. "I think you should keep it as a reminder there's still magic in the world, even during these hard times."

Sophie's eyes widened. "Did you keep it?"

"I did," the old lady said, a soft smile playing on her lips. "That doll became my most treasured possession. It reminded me, even in the darkest times, there is light and hope. It was a symbol of kindness, a reminder that magic can come in the most unexpected forms."

Sophie sat back, deep in thought, her eyes glistening with unshed tears. The story had stirred something within her, a flicker of belief, of wonder. "Do you think it was magic that brought my reindeer back to me? I thought I had lost it forever."

"Absolutely. These things are sent to us to remind us of the magic of Christmas when we start to lose the faith. If you ignore the signs, then the magic of Christmas could be lost forever, as it is with a lot of adults."

"Do you think that is what's happened to my mum? Has she lost the Christmas faith?"

"It is possible," the old lady replied, her face saddened.

The old lady reached for a small, worn photo album on the table beside her. She flipped through it, stopping at a faded black-and-white photo.

"Here," she said, handing the album to Sophie. "This photo is me. You can see me holding the doll."

Sophie took the album, her eyes falling upon the image of a young girl, no older than herself, holding the doll. It looked exactly as the old lady had described.

"It's beautiful," Sophie whispered, tracing the outline of the photo with her finger.

The old lady nodded. "I cannot remember what happened to the doll. It was such a long time ago."

"You haven't opened your present yet," Sophie said with a big smile.

The old lady picked up her gift and carefully unwrapped it. There was a plain brown cardboard box, no writing or markings, just a plain box. The old lady carefully lifted the lid. Her eyes lit up, and the biggest smile graced her face. The old lady reached inside and pulled out a doll, not just any doll. It was the very doll she had as a child. A single tear fell from her eyes as she held the doll close to her chest. Sophie's eyes widened as her mouth fell open in astonishment. A cold shiver now ran down Sophie's back. Sophie's voice trembled slightly, a mixture of excitement and nervousness. "Is it really the same doll?" she asked, her eyes never leaving the doll.

The old lady turned to Sophie, her eyes now brimming with tears, yet shining with a deep, heartfelt joy. "It is," she whispered; her voice laced with emotion. "Oh, my dear, this is... this is more than just a doll. This was my companion during the loneliest days of my childhood. I never thought I'd see her again." Her fingers gently brushed over the doll's hair. "How did you find her, Sophie?"

Sophie's astonishment turned to confusion. "I... I didn't. I came here to help Santa deliver the presents."

The old lady looked at the doll, then at Sophie, a sense of wonder enveloping her. "It's a miracle," she murmured. "It has to be. It's a Christmas miracle."

Sophie nodded, her own heart racing with a mix of confusion and amazement. The old lady hugged the doll closer, a tearful smile on her face. "Magic or not, this is the best gift I could have ever received. It's not just a doll, Sophie. It's a piece of my past, a token of my childhood joys and sorrows. It's like having a part of me returned after all these years."

Sophie watched the joy on the old lady's face as she held back her own tears. The old lady leaned over and gave Sophie a hug.

"Thank you, my dear. Thank you for giving me one of the best Christmases ever."

The room, with its festive decorations and the scent of Christmas wafting through the air, seemed to embody the very essence of what they were talking about. As Sophie watched the other residents open their gifts, their faces glowed with appreciation. Something in Sophie's heart lifted. The day

36

gradually turned into early evening. Sophie helped the residents with their Christmas preparations, her heart lighter, her mind filled with the old lady's story. When it was time for Sophie to leave, she hugged the old lady goodbye. "Thank you for sharing your story with me," she said.

The old lady hugged her back. "And thank you for listening, my dear. Remember, the spirit of Christmas is always with you, as long as you keep it alive in your heart."

Sophie and Lily stepped out into the crisp winter night, the stars twinkling above them. Sophie looked up at the sky, thinking about the old lady's story, thinking about the mysterious doll, and the true magic of Christmas. She smiled, a sense of wonder and belief warming her heart. As they walked home, Sophie turned to Lily. "I'm still not sure about Santa being real, but there is definitely something odd happening."

The December air was crisp and cold as Lily and Sophie walked home through the snow-laden streets. The Christmas lights strung across the lampposts twinkled merrily, but Sophie seemed indifferent to their charm.

"I just think we're too old for all this Santa stuff," Sophie said, kicking at the snow on the pavement.

Lily, wrapped tightly in her scarf, looked at her best friend with a mix of disbelief and sadness. "But Sophie, the magic of Christmas is real! Even you said strange things have been happening, your reindeer, for example, and that old lady's doll."

Sophie shrugged. "It was strange, that's true; I just don't know what to believe anymore."

Just then, Lily's attention was caught by a flicker of movement near a frost-covered hedge. She stopped and stared; her mouth slightly agape.

"What is it, Lily?" Sophie asked, following her gaze but seeing nothing.

"There... Do you see him?" Lily pointed towards the hedge.

Sophie squinted her eyes. "See who?"

Lily's voice dropped to a whisper. "An elf... right there!"

Sophie looked again, but all she saw was the hedge and the falling snow. "I don't see any elf, Lily. Are you okay?"

Before Lily could respond, a soft, high-pitched voice spoke to her. "Lily, I'm here for a very special reason."

Lily's eyes widened as a small, sprightly elf with pointy ears, wearing a green and red outfit, stepped out from behind the hedge. He had a jolly smile and carried a tiny lantern which emitted a soft, golden glow.

Sophie looked back and forth between Lily and where she was pointing. "Lily, I really don't see anyone."

Lily stood rooted to the spot, her gaze locked onto the figure that only she could see. The elf, a diminutive creature, aglow with an otherworldly light, seemed to radiate the essence of Christmas itself. To Lily, his appearance was not just a mere occurrence but a profound affirmation of the beliefs she held dear. The elf's presence was as real to her as the snow beneath her feet, a vivid symbol of the enchantment and wonder which permeated the Christmas season. This was not merely an encounter with a mythical being; it was a call to embark on a journey of discovery, an invitation to explore the depths of Christmas magic and its capacity to inspire awe and joy.

The elf, with eyes twinkling like stars on a clear winter night, represented a bridge between the physical and the mystical worlds, the seen and the unseen. His sudden appearance was a powerful reminder that the magic of Christmas was boundless, capable of touching hearts and changing minds in the most extraordinary ways. For Lily, this was an opportunity not only to witness the wonders of Christmas herself but also to share this miracle with Sophie. It was a chance to demonstrate that the spirit of Christmas was still alive and well, manifesting itself in moments of beauty and mystery which defied logical explanation. As Lily watched, mesmerised, the elf gestured with a small, elegant hand, beckoning her to listen closely. The elf's laughter was a delightful sound, reminiscent of the tinkling of tiny, distant bells. It was a sound which seemed to resonate with the very essence of Christmas.

"How is it that I can see you and Sophie can't?"

"That's because you are a true believer." he explained with a twinkle in his eye. "I'm Jingles, I've come from the North Pole, and I need your help." Jingles gave a little bow.

Lily, still in a state of awe and disbelief, watched the elf with wide eyes. Jingles, despite his small stature, carried an air of importance and a certain mystical charm. He was clad in traditional elf attire, a green tunic with red trim, a hat with a jingling bell at its tip, and tiny boots which seemed to leave no footprints in the snow. Jingles was not just any elf; he was a part of an ancient and secret order of Christmas elves known only to those who truly believed in the magic of Christmas. These elves, invisible to the sceptical eye, were guardians of the Christmas spirit, working tirelessly to spread joy and maintain the wonder of the season.

As Jingles stood before Lily, his presence was a testament to her own belief and her connection to the magic of Christmas. He needed her help, not just because she could see him, but because her belief represented the very power which could make the impossible, possible. His arrival marked the beginning of an extraordinary adventure.

"My help?" Lily asked, her voice filled with awe.

"Yes," Jingles said, nodding. "Your friend Sophie has lost her belief in the magic of Christmas, and so has her mum. We need to help them find it again."

Lily turned to Sophie, who was looking more confused than ever. "Sophie, he says we need to help you believe again."

Sophie frowned, looking at the empty space. "Lily, are you sure you're feeling okay?"

Lily smiled, a plan forming in her mind. "Just trust me, Sophie. Let's go on an adventure. If you don't see the magic by the end, I'll never talk about it again."

Sophie sighed. "Okay, Lily. I'll give it a try."

Jingles grinned, clapping his hands. "Wonderful! Your first adventure awaits. Follow this clue." he said, handing her a card, it read:

The lantern is missing, whisked away by the past,
To find it again, you must be fast.
In the tearooms it hides, within a photo's frame.
Seek out Mrs James, she knows the game.
Ask for her aid with a word and a glance,
Together search for the photo and take your chance.
In that snapshot of time, the lantern does wait,
Find it and you can celebrate your fate.

Jingles winked, and clicked his fingers. He vanished in a puff of smoke and twinkling glittery stars.

"It's the start of our Christmas mission," Lily exclaimed, her voice brimming with excitement. "Come on, we've got work to do!"

Together they set off, the envelope secure in Lily's grip; ready to discover the magic which awaited them.

"Where did you get that?" Said Sophie, curiously looking at the envelope.

"Jingle's the elf gave it to me."

Chapter 4

It was early Sunday morning, Lily and Sophie stood outside Mrs James' Tearooms, the chilly winter air nipping at their cheeks. In Lily's hand was the note from their mysterious Christmas elf. The instruction on the card read; "Light the way in the hidden garden behind Mrs James' Tea rooms."

Lily read the clue aloud once more:

The lantern is missing, whisked away by the past,
To find it again, you must be fast.
In the tearooms it hides, within a photo's frame,
Seek out Mrs James, she knows the game.
Ask for her aid with a word and a glance,
Together search for the photo and take your chance.
In that snapshot of time, the lantern does wait,
Find it and you can celebrate your fate.

Their eyes sparkled with excitement and curiosity, as they stepped into the quaint tearoom, the creaking of the door, and the sound of the bell above the door announcing their arrival. A warm, inviting atmosphere greeted them. Vintage decorations adorned the cosy interior, creating a nostalgic and welcoming feeling. The walls lined with rustic wooden shelves, brimming with an array of colourful tea canisters, each meticulously labelled with charming handwritten tags.

The air filled with an array of fragrances. The dominant aroma was a blend of various coffees. Intermingling with these, the sweet smells of freshly baked pastries and scones, their buttery scent promising a delightful treat.

The shop exuded an old-world charm with a large, antique-looking tea set displayed in one corner. The gentle clinking of porcelain cups and saucers resonated softly as the customers enjoyed their drinks. All seated at small, intimate tables, each draped in lace tablecloths and adorned with a beautiful petite vase of fresh flowers.

Near the counter, a display of homemade cakes and biscuits tempted the customers. The rich smell of chocolate cake, the spicy aroma of gingerbread, and the sweet scent of berry tarts forming a tantalising bouquet. Mrs James was standing behind the counter. The 55-year-old owner of the tea rooms, carrying the charm and grace of experience in her every feature. Of medium height and with a comforting presence, she was often seen with a gentle smile gracing her lips. Her hair, showing the elegance of age, was a soft blonde, usually styled in a practical yet stylish bun which spoke of the no-nonsense approach she had to her business.

Her face, lined with the subtle marks of time, reflected the years of joy and challenges she had encountered. Around her eyes, crinkles appearing whenever she smiled or laughed, which was often, adding to her warm and approachable demeanour. Her eyes themselves were a subtle blue, clear and bright, reflecting both the wisdom and the kindness she extended to all who visit her tea room.

"Hello Mrs James," said Lily, before continuing, "We have a mystery to solve, and we need your help."

"My help." said Mrs James warmly, "well, I will try."

Lily took a deep breath. "Do you have a picture with a lantern in it?"

Mrs James thought for a second, "Why, yes I have, It's there." She replied, pointing to the back wall, "What mystery do you have to solve?" she asked politely.

Lily turned and smiled. "We have to find the lantern and put it back where it belongs?"

"That old lantern has been missing for years. I doubt it still exists." she said thoughtfully.

Sophie looked at the old black and white photograph, and then at Mrs James, "What is so special about this lantern?"

"Let me tell you a story from many, many Christmases ago, a story which has been passed down in my family for generations. It's about the magic lantern and how it brought an extraordinary wonder to our tea rooms' garden each Christmas, back in the Edwardian period. You see, my grandparents owned these tea rooms long before I did, and they were always looking for ways to make Christmas extra special for the village. The garden, with its quaint paths and cosy nooks and cranny's, was already a beloved spot, but during Christmas, it was transformed into something out of a fairy tale. One Christmas, my grandfather, ever the innovator, incorporated the magic lantern into the Christmas festivities. The magic lantern was a marvel at the time, capable of projecting enchanting images which could take your breath away. But my grandfather had a grander vision. He wanted to use it to create something magical, something the village folk would talk about for years to come. So, on Christmas Eve, as the villagers gathered in the garden, sipping on hot cider and nibbling on gingerbread, the magic lantern show began. But this was no ordinary show. As the images from the lantern danced across the garden walls and trees, something wondrous started to happen.

With each picture projected by the lantern, ice sculptures began to appear in the garden as if by magic. There were ice reindeers, sleighs, angels, and even a life-sized Santa Claus. Each sculpture was intricately detailed and glowed softly under the winter night sky. It was as if the images from the lantern had come to life in ice. Lily and Sophie were wide-eyed with wonder. No one knew how my grandfather had managed it. Some said it was a trick of the light, others whispered of a secret pact with a winter fairy. But my grandfather, he just smiled and winked, never revealing his secret. Each year thereafter, the magic lantern show with the mysterious ice sculptures became a cherished Christmas tradition in the village. People came from far and wide to see the spectacle, and for a few magical hours, the garden became a major attraction for the village. Now, many years have passed, and the magic lantern is no longer with us, it has been lost in the passage of time. So, that, my dears, is the tale of how the magic lantern brought a touch of enchantment to our tea rooms' garden at Christmas. Mind you, the garden was a lot bigger back then; it has been built on since those days."

"Wow, that's amazing. That sounds like real Christmas magic." Lily replied.

The girls studied the picture. "Where is this garden, Mrs James?" asked Sophie.

Mrs James looked at the girls, curiosity written all over her face. "It's at the back of the shop."

Lily's eyes widened in anticipation. "Would it be possible to have a look in the garden, please?"

"I suppose so, but there is nothing there now. There is a passageway on the right of the shop. You can go down there."

"Thank you." Said the girls in unison and left the shop.

They went through the passage and into the snow-covered garden.

"Where do you think it is?" Sophie asked. She kept breathing into the air, forming little clouds in the cold air.

Lily pointed to a narrow, snow-covered path barely visible under the blanket of snow. "Maybe it's over there," she suggested, her voice filled with adventure.

The two friends, bundled in their warmest winter coats, set off across the garden. As they walked down the path, their boots made the snow crunch, and the crisp winter air resonated with the distant sound of Christmas carols.

The girls entered the garden. The bustle of the village faded, replaced by a serene silence. As they moved further into the garden, the large walled garden loomed around them. Ivy covered the walls, twining around every stone and crevice. Snow blanketed everything in a soft, white layer. In one corner, a large stone statuette stood against a wall, almost hidden by the snow and ivy. The path wound its way through the garden, leading them to a wrought-iron gate. They approached the gate cautiously. It looked old and heavy, its once-black paint now chipped and rusted. The girls braced themselves and pushed the gate hard. It protested loudly, the rusty hinges groaning and screeching in defiance. With a final heave, the gate creaked open, revealing another garden beyond.

This new garden was just as enchanting. The path continued, flanked by snow-covered bushes and trees. Three stone statues stood along the path, each draped in ivy and snow. The statues seemed to watch the girls as they moved forward, their stone faces serene and timeless. They continued down the path, the crunch of snow under their boots the only sound in the peaceful garden. The statues stood silent and still, guardians of this winter wonderland.

"The lantern must have been in here somewhere," Lily whispered, her eyes scanning the garden.

They searched amidst the stone sculptures, their hands occasionally brushing against the cold ice. Finally, Sophie's mitten'd hand felt something different, the smooth surface of the stone plinth hidden under a blanket of ivy. She pulled at the ivy to reveal the icy stone. "This has to be where it stood."

"But where should we begin our search for the lantern? We haven't been given any clues for that part."

Lily recoiled in surprise as Jingles, the Christmas elf, materialised on the plinth. Despite its high pitch, there was a warmth and cheerfulness in the elf's voice, which added a touch of whimsy and charm to his character. He danced in the air. "So, you've discovered the resting place of the lantern," he said in a playful tone. "Now, the quest to find the lantern itself awaits you."

Sophie looked at Lily as she started to speak to the stone plinth. "Jingles, you made me jump. Can you give us a clue as to where it might be hidden?"

"Hmm, let me think." Said Jingles, smiling.

"Is he here now?" asked Sophie.

"Yes, he's thinking about giving us a clue to find the lantern."

Jingles paused for a moment, deep in thought. He crossed his left arm in front of his body and placed his chin between the thumb and forefinger of his right hand, resting his right elbow on his left arm. He looked up at Lily. Without moving his arm, he released hold of his chin and pointed at Lily. "Alright, here's your clue." Jingles took a deep breath. Then recited the clue.

"In the heart of the village where laughter resounds,
Seek where the festive tunes of the carollers abounds.
Near the tallest tree, bathed in moonlight,
Look closely at its base, on this cold winter's night.
Hidden from view, where shadows and whispers play,
The lantern lies waiting, lost from the light of day.
But remember, dear seeker, as you embark on this quest,
To find the hidden lantern, your wits must be at their best."

Jingles thrust both hands high into the air. A burst of glittery stars enveloped his body, then in a flash, he disappeared.

"He's gone again." sighed Lily.

"Did he give us a clue?"

"Yes, it's strange, but I can remember it perfectly." Lily Cleared her throat.

"In the heart of the village where laughter resounds,
Seek where the festive tunes of the carollers abounds.
Near the tallest tree, bathed in moonlight,
Look closely at its base, on this cold winter's night.
Hidden from view, where shadows and whispers play,
The lantern lies waiting, lost from the light of day.
But remember, dear seeker, as you embark on this quest,
To find the hidden lantern, your wits must be at their best."

Sophie listened intently to the clue. "In the heart of the village, that must be the village square."

The two girls made their way as fast as they could to the village square. On arrival, they noticed the square was empty, just the odd villager going about their business.

"There's no one here singing carols?"

"The tallest tree must be the Christmas tree over there." Sophie pointed to the tall Christmas tree standing in the middle of the square.

The girls raced over and searched around the tree. "There's nothing here." Cried Lily.

"It has to be," Said Sophie. "Say the clue again."

"In the heart of the village where laughter resounds,
Seek where the festive tunes of the carollers abounds.
Near the tallest tree, bathed in moonlight,
Look closely at its base, on this cold winter's night.
Hidden from view, where shadows and whispers play,
The lantern lies waiting, lost from the light of day.
But remember, dear seeker, as you embark on this quest,
To find the hidden lantern, your wits must be at their best."

Sophie gave a little sigh. "Okay, we are at the tree. We have looked all around the base... What are we missing?"

One of Sophie's neighbours walked past with her dog. "Hello Sophie, are you getting some practice in for tonight's carol concert?"

Sophie gave a small, embarrassed laugh. "No, we are just playing, Mrs Wright."

Mrs wright smiled sweetly and kept walking her dog.

"Of course," exclaimed Lily, "The lantern is lost from the light of day, and the tree is not bathed in moonlight. We need to come back when it's dark and the carol concert is on. That's what he meant by our wits must be at their best. We haven't listened to the clue properly."

Sophie exhaled and her body deflated a little as her shoulders dropped. "My mum is going to the concert tonight."

"That's okay, I can come with you. We can look around while everyone is busy singing."

Sophie nodded in agreement, and they made their way home.

Later that evening, the air filled with a crisp winter chill. Lily, Sophie, and Sophie's mum wrapped themselves in warm coats, scarves and hats as they walked towards the annual carol service. The village square was already bustling with activity, a small crowd was gathering. Each person holding a candle encased in an empty glass jar to protect its flame from the whims of the wind. The flickering candlelight cast a warm, gentle glow across the faces of the villagers who were carrying them, creating a scene which was both festive and serene.

"Mum, why are there no lights on the tree?" Sophie asked, her breath forming small clouds in the cold air as she gazed at the towering Christmas tree standing majestically in the centre of the village square.

Her mum smiled softly, a hint of nostalgia in her eyes. "The festivities in the village are not as good as they used to be. It's been quite some time since this tree had any lights on it," Sophie's mum began, a reflective tone in her voice. "The village festivities aren't what they used to be, and they've been diminishing each year. I guess people have started to forget the magic that once lit up our winters. You see, years ago, this village was known far and wide for its Christmas spirit. The tree would be adorned with twinkling lights, and the air would be filled with the sound of carols and laughter. But as time went by, things changed. People got busier, and slowly, the grandeur of our Christmas celebrations faded. It's as if the village has lost a bit of its sparkle, and with it, the tradition of lighting up the tree has faded too. Now, it stands there, tall, and beautiful in its own right, but without the lights, it's like a symbol of how our community has changed. I sometimes wonder if we'll ever see those lights again, or if the joyous spirit of those days will just remain a part of our past now." Sophie's mum sighed softly, a hint of nostalgia in her eyes as she looked out at the unlit tree.

Sophie looked up at the tree, its branches silhouetted against the starry night sky. In the candlelight, the tree seemed to possess its own serene, unadorned majesty.

"Yeah, it's like it's standing there as a symbol, reminding us of all the Christmases that have come and gone, and of those still to be celebrated." Lily observed, her eyes shimmering with the reflection of her own flickering candle within the jar she carefully held in her hands.

The carol service began. The harmonious voices of the villagers singing Christmas carols enveloped them in a warm, Christmassy feeling. Standing there, the tree acted as a silent sentinel, observing the age-old traditions and the timeless joy of the season. The moment felt magical, as if the tree, in its unlit state, held many secrets and stories of Christmases past.

Lily and Sophie walked around the tree singing carols. The moon cast a soft glow over the snow-covered ground, making the unlit tree stand out against the night sky.

Lily turned to Sophie and whispered, "Okay, so the clue says it's near the tallest tree, bathed in moonlight. This is the tallest tree, and the moon is out, shining on it."

Sophie nodded, looking around. "And it mentions shadows and whispers... Maybe it's hidden somewhere not obvious, like behind the tree or in a hollow?"

Sophie walked around the tree, her eyes scanning the ground. Lily joined her, peering into the shadows. "I can't see anything, can you?" she whispered.

Sophie looked at the base of the tree. Something glinted in the moonlight. She nudged Lily and pointed to the base of the tree.

"Sophie, what are you doing?" exclaimed her mum.

Sophie pretended she didn't hear her and knelt down, brushing snow from the base of the tree. "Hey, what's this?" she muttered, feeling something under her fingers.

Lily crouched beside her. "Is it the lantern?"

Sophie pulled out a green and gold lantern, hidden among the tree roots and snow. It was ornately crafted, with intricate patterns etched into its surface. "We found it!" Sophie exclaimed. "This has to be it!" she continued, holding up the lantern.

Lily's eyes lit up with excitement. "This has to be it! The lost lantern from the clue!"

They looked at each other, a sense of achievement and wonder in their eyes. "We did it, Lily! Your wits and our teamwork," Sophie said, a smile spreading across her face.

Holding the lantern between them, they felt a sense of magic in the air, their hearts filled with the joy of their Christmas adventure. Jingles reappeared, "Well done. You cracked the clue. Now for some Christmas magic, ask Sophie to count down from 10 loudly."

As the last notes of a carol faded into the crisp winter air, leaving a hush over the gathered crowd, Lily leaned closer to Sophie. The twinkling of the candles in jars held in people's hands cast a soft glow on their faces as they readied for the next carol.

"Sophie, Jingles told me something important," Lily whispered urgently. "You need to count down from 10, really loud."

Sophie looked puzzled. "But why? What's going to happen?"

"I don't know, but Jingles was very clear. Just trust me on this," Lily urged, her eyes sparkling with a mix of excitement and mystery.

Sophie hesitated for a moment, then took a deep breath. With all the conviction she could muster, she began, her voice ringing clear in the hushed square. "10, 9, 8, 7, 6"

People around them turned, curiously watching Sophie as she counted down. Sophie's voice echoed. "5, 4, 3, 2..." The moment Sophie reached '1', there was an unmistakable sense of anticipation in the air. Jingles, still visible only to Lily, snapped his fingers. In an instant, the large, unlit Christmas tree burst into life with beautiful, twinkling Christmas lights. The lights weaved through the branches in a dazzling display, bathing it in a warm, festive glow.

Gasps and murmurs of astonishment rippled through the crowd. "The tree! It's lit up!" exclaimed someone in the crowd, their voice a mixture of surprise and delight.

Sophie's mum, standing beside them, her eyes wide with wonder, murmured, "I haven't seen the tree lit up like this in

49

years. It's... it's beautiful. How on earth did you two do that? Has it anything to do with you and whatever it is you are holding?"

Sophie nodded, "I think so." She whispered.

Sophie's mum raised an eyebrow, a look of puzzlement crossing her face. "What are you saying? I'm not quite following," she said, clearly bewildered.

As Sophie stared at the tree in awe, she felt a warm glow in her heart. "Lily, did you know this was going to happen?" she asked, her voice a mix of astonishment and joy.

Lily looked the tree with a loving smile, squeezed Sophie's hand. "No, Jingles did not tell me that part," she whispered, her eyes reflecting the newly lit lights of the tree.

"Okay, you two, I need to understand what's happening here. And just who might this Jingles be?" The words were curious, gentle, but firm.

Lily and Sophie, looking a bit nervous, glanced at each other. Sophie took a small step forward, her voice soft but clear. "Well, you might find this hard to believe, but some really odd things have been happening lately. I can't quite put my finger on why, but it has something to do with Christmas, and maybe even Santa Claus."

The response came with a chuckle, "Oh, my! Let me guess, Jingles must be some kind of magical elf, right?" Sophie's mum replied.

Sophie let out a big sigh, almost as if she was letting go of a secret. "Yes, he's a magical Christmas elf. But the strangest thing is, it seems Lily is the only one who can see him."

The reply was again gentle but firm. "Perhaps he's just a character from a story in your head. Santa is not a real person."

Sophie spoke up, her voice filled with excitement. "But it's not just a story mum! There have been so many unusual things happening. Like this," she said, holding up a beautiful, shiny lantern. "It's been missing for a long time, and Jingles told us exactly where and when we could find it."

"And who filled your heads with tales of a missing lantern? It looks perfectly new to me," came the puzzling question.

Both girls answered together, "Mrs James told us about it!"

As the girls were discussing the mysterious lantern, Mrs James strolled by. Her ears perked up when she heard her name being mentioned. She paused, turned around, and asked with a twinkle in her eye, "Did someone just call out for me?"

The moment they saw Mrs James, Lily, and Sophie's faces burst into bright smiles. "Mrs James, look!" Sophie said with glee, raising the lantern high for her to see. "We found your lantern, the very same one you've been telling us about, right?"

They all gathered around, their eyes wide in anticipation, eager to hear what Mrs James would say. "Well now, it does look like the lantern from the picture. But how on earth did you find it, and in such perfect condition too?" she asked, her voice filled with wonder.

"It was Jingles who guided us," Lily explained, her voice bubbling with excitement. "He told us exactly where and when to find it. It felt like real magic!"

Sophie's mum let out a soft chuckle. "Magic, indeed."

Lily chimed in earnestly, "It's all true. Jingles said we need to return the lantern to its rightful place to see the magic unfold."

Sophie's mother, a nonbeliever, sighed. "I'm sorry, Mrs James, but this sounds like typical children's fantasies."

Mrs James, always full of surprises, had a twinkle in her eye. "Since Christmas is almost here, and it's a magical time, let's all go to the garden behind my shop and put the lantern there. I'm quite curious to see what might happen if it's returned to its original spot. Besides, the girls found this lantern, after all?"

"Mrs James, I'm not sure if we should encourage this kind of thing," said Sophie's mother, a bit unsure of the situation.

Mrs James smiled warmly. "What harm can it do? At the very least, I'll have a beautiful lantern for my garden. And how about this, I'll make us all a delightful treat, hot chocolate with whipped cream and marshmallows, a perfect Christmas indulgence?"

The girls' eyes sparkled at the mention of hot chocolate. "Yes, please!" they exclaimed in unison, their excitement uncontrollable.

Sophie's mother, seeing the joy in her daughter's eyes, relented with a smile. "Well, that does sound very generous of you, Mrs James."

Mrs James waved off the compliment. "Oh, it's nothing at all. Consider it my treat for the season." Her words filled the air with a sense of warmth and anticipation as everyone prepared to witness the magic which awaited them in the garden. All except that is, Sophie's mum, who was sceptical about the whole thing.

"Girls, I don't want you disappointed if nothing happens," said Sophie's mum, preparing the ground for what she expected to be the outcome.

They journeyed towards Mrs James' cosy tearoom, their footsteps rhythmically crunching on the crisp, freshly fallen snow. The air was chilly and invigorating.

Upon arriving at the quaint tearoom, Mrs James, ever the thoughtful hostess, proposed a splendid idea. "Before we venture into the garden to return the lantern to its rightful place, let's whip up some delicious hot chocolate. It will help keep us toasty and warm while we're outside in this cold air," she suggested with a smile.

Her suggestion was met with nods of agreement and excited smiles, especially from Lily and Sophie. The idea of drinking a steamy cup of hot chocolate with whipped cream and marshmallows made them feel warm and cosy even before they tasted it. It seemed like it would be the perfect accompaniment to their magical outdoor adventure.

Together, they all bustled into the tearoom, the aroma of spices and baked goods greeting them. Mrs James led them to the kitchen, where everyone pitched in to help make the hot chocolate. With mugs steaming in their hands, they ventured into the garden led by Mrs James, who lit the way with a very large and bright torch. Once again, Lily and Sophie found themselves in front of the wrought-iron gate. Mrs James pushed it open as it squealed on its rusty hinges.

"Now, where do we place the lantern?" asked Mrs James, wondering aloud, looking around for any clue.

They wandered through the garden; Sophie carefully placed the lantern on the pedestal and opened its little door for Mrs James to light a candle inside it. As she did, something magical happened. The light from the lantern cast a warm glow over the garden. Several ice sculptures began to appear and shimmer with a gentle light of their own, as if infused with magical life. They all stood in awe, watching the spectacle unfold before their eyes. Sophie's mum and Mrs James could not believe what was happening. Both Lily and Sophie watched with their mouths wide open.

"What?... How?" Stuttered Sophie's mum. "This is not possible. There is no such thing as magic."

In that moment, as the garden transformed before their eyes, a complex rush of emotions enveloped both Sophie's mum and Mrs James. Sophie's mum, a self-professed non-believer in magic and in Santa, was engulfed in a mixture of disbelief and bewilderment, her rational mind struggling to make sense of the miraculous scene unfolding before her. The emergence of the shimmering ice sculptures, conjured by the mere lighting of a candle, challenged her steadfast views.

Mrs James, on the other hand, experienced a profound sense of wonder mixed with a nostalgic affirmation. Having grown up with tales of the magic lantern and its enchanting Christmas displays, she had always harboured a deep-seated belief in the season's magic and the mysteries it could unveil. Seeing the ice sculptures materialise, made her heart swell with a joyous validation of the stories she cherished since childhood. Yet, there was also an element of surprise, a delightful astonishment at witnessing such magic in reality, a spectacle she only ever imagined in her fondest dreams.

Both women, despite their differing perspectives on the existence of magic, were united in their awe. The spectacle transcended their individual beliefs. Captivating them with its beauty and the sheer impossibility of what was happening. For a moment, the line between reality and fantasy blurred. Leaving them both in a shared state of wonder, reminding them that sometimes the world holds mysteries which are far beyond the realm of explanation.

The garden was like a scene from a fairytale, with ice sculptures of angels, reindeer, and snowflakes, all glistening under the light of the moon.

They noticed something else. A small golden envelope appeared at the base of the Christmas elf sculpture. Lily reached for it, her fingers trembling with anticipation. Inside, they found another note from their Christmas elf, along with a large old key. The note read; *'Discover a hidden Athenaeum, with old Christmas tales and spend the day reading stories about old village traditions now forgotten.'*

"What's that?" asked Sophie.

"It's an old key," Lily read the tag which was attached to it, "This opens the hidden ath... en... yum, thing."

"A what?" asked Sophie.

Lily showed the clue to Mrs James. "Athenaeum, it's Greek."

"What does it mean?" Asked Sophie.

"Well, the clue was left for you two. You need to find that out for yourselves."

Chapter 5

Lily and Sophie hurried to Lily's house to use her computer, their excitement growing with each step. Lily typed 'Athenaeum' into the search bar, her fingers dancing over the keys. The screen filled with various results. "Look," pointed Sophie, "It's Greek for a library. What did the note from Jingles say again? I forgot."

Lily took a note from the envelope. *"Discover a hidden Athenaeum with old Christmas tales and spend the day reading stories about old village traditions now forgotten."*

"It has to be a hidden section in the library," Sophie concluded, her eyes lighting up with realisation.

Lily nodded in agreement.

"But why would Jingles want us to find it? And how do we even begin to look for something that's hidden?" Asked Sophie.

Lily leaned back in her chair, thinking. "It's not just about finding it. Maybe it's about rediscovering something important about our village's past. The bit where it says *'old village traditions now forgotten.'*"

Sophie's eyes sparkled with intrigue. "You mean like a mystery that's been forgotten over time?"

"Exactly!" Lily said, her voice filled with enthusiasm. "And what better time to uncover forgotten stories than Christmas?"

Filled with a new sense of purpose, Lily and Sophie decided to visit the library the next day. Now the school was closed because of problems with the boiler, they had more time to complete the task. They wrapped up in their winter coats and set off through the white, snowy streets of the village.

Arriving at the library, the ever-smiling Mrs Greenwood, who was busy organising a display of colourful books, greeted Lily and Sophie. The library was warm, and with its high ceilings and rows of shelves, it was a welcome sanctuary from the chilly weather outside.

"Ah, Lily and Sophie! What brings you two here on this wintry morning?" Her eyes twinkling behind her purple-rimmed glasses.

"We're here to do some research for a project we are working on." replied Sophie, her voice echoing slightly in the spacious library.

"Well, if you need any help, you know where I am." Gesturing to the large wooden desk adorned with a quaint brass lamp.

The girls explored the library; their footsteps muffled by the thick carpet. "Where on earth do we start?" Sophie wondered aloud, her eyes scanning the endless rows of books.

"We need an old door for the key to unlock." Lily reminded her, clutching the mysterious, ornate key in her hand.

Despite their diligent search, no old doors could be found. Frustration clouded their excitement. They were just about to give up when Lily's gaze fell upon a peculiar book resting on an aged mahogany shelf, it was a large book bound in royal blue leather. Its wide spine was peculiar and seemed to whisper of hidden secrets and long-lost tales. The gold lettering embossed upon its spine glinted in the light. 'The History of Our Village'. She could hear the silent call of the letters, beckoning her to unveil the mysteries bound within.

Compelled by an unseen force, Lily reached out, her fingers trembled slightly with anticipation. The moment her fingers touched the leather, a warm sensation rushed through her. The cover felt surprisingly soft, the leather rich and inviting despite its clear age. It was as though she was touching history itself, every grain and fold affirming the book's lengthy journey through the ages. The spine was rounded and robust, a full 2 inches thick, hinting at the wealth of enthralling stories which lay within. As she lifted the book, an old, musty smell enveloped her. It was the scent of the ancient leather mixed with a hint of mustiness, suggesting pages filled with stories only whispered through time. Running her fingers over the book's spine, she discovered an unusual keyhole hidden among the embossed patterns. This was no ordinary book; it was a gateway to another realm.

Lily glanced at her friend, their eyes locking with mutual excitement. "Shall we?" she whispered, her voice a mixture of eagerness and wonder. Her friend nodded, the thrill of the unknown reflecting in their gaze. Carefully, Lily inserted the key into the book. As she turned it, a soft click echoed in the quiet library. Abruptly, the room changed. The library suddenly transformed, revealing a hidden chamber, a small candle chandelier hung from the centre of the ceiling. The two friends stepped into the newly revealed room, their eyes wide with wonder. Around them, the air felt charged with magic. It was the sort of magic that whispered of adventures and worlds beyond their own. The room, hidden from the eyes of those who walked the library's halls, was a treasure trove of secrets waiting to be discovered.

The chamber, though modest in size, exuded an aura of an ancient Greek Athenaeum, as if whispers of forgotten scholars lingered in its walls. At the heart of the room stood a carved wooden table, ornately designed with intricate patterns, flanked by two high-backed chairs that seemed to anticipate the arrival of seekers eager to unlock its secrets. The air was thick with an age-old enchantment, and dust particles floated gracefully in the rays of golden light coming from the candle chandelier. The soft glow bathed the room in a warm, almost sacred light, wrapping it in a veil of mystery and wisdom. Against the far wall, a solitary shelf held a single, ancient tome titled 'Forgotten Times.' Its leather-bound cover, adorned with faded symbols and gilded edges, was thick with a layer of dust, hinting at centuries of abandonment, as though it had patiently waited through the ages for someone worthy to unearth the secrets it concealed. The room was alive with a quiet magic, a place where past and present converged, inviting any who entered to step into the realms of myth and memory.

Yet, despite its neglected appearance, the book seemed to beckon the girls, as if it was alive with stories eager to be told. Lily reached out, her fingers brushing against the book before taking it from the shelf and placing it on the table. Sophie approached the table, her eyes wide with wonder and excitement. "Lily, do you think this book could help us with our mission?" she asked, her voice filled with hope and curiosity.

Lily, equally awe-struck by their find, nodded thoughtfully. "I think it might hold more than just help for our mission, Sophie. It might hold secrets, long forgotten, waiting to be discovered by us," she replied, her voice imbued with a sense of adventure. As they sat down, the room seemed to welcome them, wrapping them in a cocoon of warmth and mystery. The light above cast its gentle glow on the book of 'Forgotten Times,' highlighting its embossed surface. Sophie gently picked up the book and blew the dust off its cover, a cloud of particles swirling in the soft light. She carefully opened the book, her hands trembling slightly with anticipation, ready to uncover the mysteries which lay within its pages.

As Lily and Sophie turned the pages of 'Forgotten Times', they arrived at chapter one, titled 'The Dance of the Snow Fairies.' Lily read the title out aloud, and the words on the page shimmered with a magical glow, as if infused with a life of their own. The dusty old room faded around them. The room was magically transformed into the village square on a snowy night. Snowflakes danced in the air, each one unique, sparkling under the moonlight. The village square, now alive with the magic of Christmas, was adorned with festive decorations and lights, casting a warm, welcoming glow. Standing amidst the snow, the girls found themselves enveloped in thick winter cloaks, their breath twirling in the cold air. The transformation occurred in an instant, whisking them away from the Athenaeum to a whimsical winter wonderland. They were greeted by a breath-taking sight of glistening snowflakes falling gently from the sky, creating a soft carpet of white. The air was filled with a crisp, refreshing scent, carrying hints of pine and frost. As they stepped onto the powdery snow, they could feel the cold tingling in their cheeks. Their ears were delighted by the muffled sounds of laughter and the distant jingle of bells.

"Wow, look at this place," Sophie whispered, her eyes sparkling with excitement.

Lily grinned, equally mesmerised. "It's like we've stepped into the story itself," she said, her voice filled with wonder.

Together, they stepped forward, eager to explore this magical world and uncover the secrets that 'Forgotten Times' had promised.

As the snowflakes fell gently from the sky, the girls, watched in wonderment as a group of snow fairies emerged, their wings shimmering in the moonlight.

The fairies, small and delicate, danced gracefully around the village square. Their dance was elegant and synchronised. Each movement causing a swirl of snowflakes to rise and fall in a beautiful, choreographed pattern.

"Look, Lily!" Sophie exclaimed, "What are they doing?"

"They're bringing the first snow of the season." Said a voice behind them.

Lily and Sophie turned to see a snow fairy, no larger than a person's thumb, hovering behind them. Her wings glistened in the moonlight, casting tiny rainbows on the snow-covered ground.

"They're bringing the first snow of the season," the fairy repeated, her voice high, but as soft as the falling snow. "It's our most cherished tradition."

Lily, her eyes wide with wonder, asked, "Do you do this every year?"

The fairy nodded. "Yes, every year. We gather in the village square and dance to welcome the winter."

Sophie, fascinated, asked, "Why does your dance bring the snow?"

The fairy smiled. "Our dance creates a special magic. It calls upon the winter spirits to blanket the ground in snow, transforming the village into a winter wonderland."

As the fairies continued their dance, the snowfall grew heavier, the village transforming before the girls' eyes. The roof of each house now covered in thick layers of snow, and the trees stood tall and proud, their branches dusted with white.

"Why are we able to see you?" Lily wondered. "Aren't fairies supposed to be hidden from human eyes?"

"Our world is usually hidden," explained the fairy. "But the book you found, 'Forgotten Times', is a bridge between our worlds. It allows those with pure hearts to see and experience the magic."

Sophie, looked around, seeing the square was now completely transformed. "It's beautiful," she said, her voice filled with wonder.

The fairy gestured to the other fairies. "Would you like to join our dance? It's not often we have human guests."

Lily and Sophie exchanged excited glances and nodded eagerly. With a wave of the fairy's hand, they found themselves lifted into the air, their feet barely touching the snow.

As they danced, Lily and Sophie felt a joy unlike any other. They twirled and spun, their movements somehow in perfect harmony with the fairies. The snow sparkled, as if celebrating their dance. Then, one of the fairies, noticing the girls, flew over to them, radiating a soft, blue light. "Welcome, Lily and Sophie, to our dance of the season," she said in a voice as delicate as the snow.

"We're honoured to be here," Sophie replied, her eyes wide with wonder. "Your dance is beautiful."

The village square, bathed in the soft glow of the full moon, was alive with the magic of the moment. The snow continued to fall, each flake adding to the enchantment. Together, they danced with the snow fairies, each movement creating new patterns in the falling snow. They twirled, leaped, and spun, their laughter mingling with the music of the fairies' dance.

As the dance came to an end, the girls found themselves transported back to the Athenaeum, the book of 'Forgotten Times' still open on the table.

"Was that real?" Sophie asked in astonishment.

"It felt real," Lily replied, smiling.

"I can't wait to see what other adventures this book holds for us," Lily said, her eyes sparkling with excitement.

And so, with the memory of the snow fairies' dance etched in their minds, Lily and Sophie continued their journey through the pages of the book, desperate to uncover more hidden wonders.

Hoping for another adventure, Sophie leaned closer to the book. "What's the next story?" she asked, with a sparkle in her eyes.

Lily turned the page to a chapter titled 'The Enchanted Christmas Tree Forest'. As they read the first lines, the room faded away once more, it was replaced by a magical forest. Each Christmas tree displayed twinkling lights and shimmering ornaments.

"Where are we?" Sophie whispered in awe.

"In the story, I guess," Lily replied, her voice filled with excitement.

"It's a forest where every Christmas tree tells a different tale of Christmas in the village." said an invisible voice.

They approached the first tree, its lights casting a warm, golden glow. A gentle voice, as soothing as a lullaby, could be heard.

The Christmas tree, with its branches adorned in lights and ornaments, seemed to come alive as it began to recount *'The Sad Tale of Oliver'* to Sophie and Lily. The tree's voice was like a gentle whisper on the wind; Oliver was a child of the Victorian era, marked by his threadbare coat and the earnest glimmer in his youthful eyes. His family, besieged by poverty, lived on the fringes of this village, where the harsh winds of winter were felt most keenly. To aid his family, Oliver embarked on a humble quest to sell mistletoe. A symbol of love and kinship, hoping he could bring some food and warmth to their cold, sparse home.

With a large bundle of mistletoe in his tiny, chapped hands, Oliver trudged through the snowy village streets. His cheeks, reddened by the biting cold, contrasted starkly with the rest of his pale, hopeful face. He stood in the village square, right beside where I, the Christmas tree, was splendidly adorned with twinkling lights and shimmering ornaments. From my vantage point, I observed Oliver's day unfold, a day marked by utter disregard and unrelenting cold.

Villagers bustled by, absorbed in their festive preparations, their laughter, and chatter creating a symphony of life around the unobtrusive boy. Oliver's voice, tender and hopeful, was drowned out by the cacophony of the season's joy. "Mistletoe for sale!" he would shout, but his voice barely audible over the jingle of sleigh bells and the laughter of the people as they passed. But no one stopped; no one noticed the boy with eyes reflecting a fading hope.

As twilight approached, the cold deepened its merciless grip. The village square emptied, leaving Oliver alone in the shadow of my boughs. His small frame shivered uncontrollably, and his eyes, once bright with hope, now flickered with the onset of despair. The night claimed the square, and with it, Oliver's last vestige of warmth.

The following morning, as the village awoke to a day of merriment, a grim discovery was made in a run-down barn at the edge of the village. Oliver, overcome by the unforgiving cold, lay there, as still as the winter itself, his bundle of unsold mistletoe clutched tightly to his chest. The whole village was enveloped in a shroud of sorrow; grief replaced joy, and regret gnawed at the hearts of those who had walked past him.

In a surge of collective guilt and sadness, the villagers banded together. They donated funds for Oliver's funeral and his bereaved family, hoping to offer some solace in their time of unimaginable loss. A special funeral was held, one befitting a fallen son of the village. The entire village came to bid farewell to the boy they once ignored, with tears and whispered apologies.

To honour his memory, a special service was initiated. Every Christmas Eve, the villagers would gather around his grave to remember Oliver. They would share stories of kindness and generosity, pledging to never let another soul suffer Oliver's fate.

Over time, memories faded. Leaving an empty void, like the desolate branches of trees in late autumn.

The once solemn tradition of remembering Oliver on Christmas Eve slowly vanished into the annals of time. New generations came, unaware of the boy who once sold mistletoe, and the tragedy which befell him, and of the promise the village once made.

I, the Christmas tree, however, remained a silent witness to the passage of time. Each year, as I stood adorned in the village square, I held Oliver's story close to my heart. I remembered the boy with the hopeful eyes and the tragic end he met. I remembered the village's fleeting remorse and the unkept promises. And on each Christmas Eve, as the snow gently fell, I whispered Oliver's story to the night, hoping the winds would carry his tale to those who still had the heart to listen.

In this village, joy and celebration continued to thrive, but hidden beneath the festive lights and merry songs, there lingered a forgotten tale of a boy named Oliver. It was a reminder of the fragility of life, the importance of kindness, and the enduring memory of a magical Christmas tree who never forgot to tell his story.

Sophie's eyes welled up. "That's a sad story. We need to do something about this when we get back." Lily nodded in agreement. They moved through the forest listening to more stories, some happy, some sad. As Sophie and Lily approached the final tree in the Enchanted Christmas Tree Forest, its branches glowing with red and green lights, a voice greeted them. It was as gentle as the falling snow. This tree was about to share *'The Tale of the Gift-Giving Robin'*.

"The most generous creature in our village was not a person but a small robin," the tree began, its voice soft and soothing. "This robin, with its bright red breast and cheerful chirp, was beloved by all in the village."

Sophie, her eyes sparkling, leaned in closer. "A robin who gives gifts! How special!"

The tree continued, "Each Christmas, this little bird would embark on a heartwarming mission. It flew around the village, gathering small items: a lost button, a shiny berry, a perfectly smooth pebble. Each item, though small, was chosen with care."

Lily, touched by the robin's thoughtfulness, whispered, "It's like it knew just what to give."

"Yes," the tree agreed. "The robin had a knack for finding just the right gift for each villager. A lost earring would find its way back to its owner. A shiny acorn would end up in the hands of a child who loved to collect them, and a sprig of holly would appear on a windowsill to brighten someone's day."

Sophie's face lit up with joy. "It wasn't about the size of the gift, but the thought behind it!"

"Exactly," said the tree. "The robin taught everyone in the village the true spirit of Christmas. It wasn't about grand gestures or expensive gifts. It was about the simple acts of kindness, the joy of giving, and the happiness brought by a thoughtful gesture."

Lily, deeply moved, added, "It shows anyone can bring joy, no matter how small they are or what little they have."

"The robin became a symbol of the village's Christmas spirit," the tree concluded. "Its legacy of giving and kindness continued to inspire the villagers, reminding them the heart of Christmas lies in the joy of giving."

As the story ended, Sophie and Lily found themselves back in the room, the enchanting glow of the forest still lingering in their eyes.

"That was amazing," Sophie exclaimed, her voice filled with wonder. "Each tree had its own story, happy or sad , each had its own magic."

Lily nodded, her heart full of the Christmas spirit. "It's like the entire forest was alive with the magic of Christmas. And each story was a lesson about the true meaning of the season."

Sophie, her eyes still alight with the fascination of the tales, said, "I'll never forget all these stories. They've made this Christmas even more special."

Lily smiled, agreeing. "Yes, and we have this book to thank for this magical journey."

As they closed the book, Sophie said, "These stories... they're not just tales. They feel real, like they're part of the village's history. We must make some notes and bring back some of these traditions."

"Yes, that's exactly what we should do," Lily added, a smile spreading across her face.

Sophie looked at Lily, her eyes twinkling with the joy of the season. "Have we got time for one more story?" she asked eagerly.

Lily glanced at her watch and nodded, her own excitement mirroring Sophie's. "Yes, I think so," she replied, reopening the book with an air of anticipation.

Turning the page, Lily's eyes lit up. "The Starlight Procession," she announced, a large grin spreading across her face.

The girls leaned in, their imaginations ready to be whisked away once more. As they read about 'The Starlight Procession', the room faded again, and the sights and sounds of a bygone era replacing it.

They found themselves amidst villagers on a snowy Christmas Eve, each person holding a handmade lantern. The warm glow of the candles flickering in the crisp night air, casting a soft light on the snow-covered streets.

Sophie, her eyes wide with wonder, whispered, "It's like we've stepped back in time."

Lily, equally amazed, nodded. "Look at the lanterns, Sophie! Every single one is different."

"Indeed, each lantern was a work of art, crafted with care and decorated with intricate designs which were special to the person who made it," said a mysterious voice. The girls looked all around, but there was no one near them.

"Who was that?" asked Sophie.

"I don't know. Was that you Jingles?"

The voice came no more. "Strange." Said Lily, scratching her head in puzzlement.

They watched as the villagers, wrapped in warm cloaks and scarves, moved slowly through the streets, their faces illuminated by the gentle candlelight.

The soft hum of carols filled the air, a gentle harmonious backdrop to the procession. The melodies were both familiar and new, evoking a sense of timelessness and peace.

Sophie, feeling the warmth of the candle in her hand, said softly, "This is beautiful, Lily."

Lily, her voice filled with emotion, replied, "It's more than that. It's like we're part of their tradition."

As they walked, they noticed the smiles and nods of the villagers, a silent acknowledgment of their shared experience. The procession wound its way through the village, past houses adorned with wreaths and ribbons, each window aglow with the light of Christmas.

Sophie, feeling the magic of the moment, said, "I can feel the warmth, not just from the candles, but from the people. It's like the glow from these lanterns is lighting up their hearts."

"And ours too," Lily added, her heart full of Christmas magic. "This procession, it's a symbol of togetherness, of sharing the light of Christmas with each other."

As the procession ended, the villagers gathered in the village square, placing their lanterns together to form a radiant display. The combined light of the lanterns was breathtaking, a symbol of unity and hope.

Sophie and Lily, standing hand in hand, took in the scene, the memory etching itself into their hearts.

The story concluded, and the girls found themselves back in the Athenaeum once more, the warmth of the procession still lingering within them.

"That was amazing," Sophie exclaimed, her voice brimming with excitement. "The Starlight Procession... it's like a... like a journey of togetherness."

Lily nodded, her eyes shining. "And a reminder that the light of Christmas can bring us all together, and remain gleaming in our hearts."

Sophie and Lily knew they had to carry the magic of *'The Starlight Procession'* to the village. A timeless reminder of the warmth and unity which defines the spirit of Christmas.

"We need to speak to your mum Sophie, and Mrs James, too. They witnessed the magic in the garden. Perhaps they can help us with our own Starlight Procession.

Chapter 6

Lily and Sophie stared at the book, then at each other. They read one more story. The title of the next story was *'The Midnight Chime of Wishes.'*

"I wonder what this one is about?" said Lily, curiosity written all over her face.

Lily read out loud, "In the heart of the village stood an ancient bell known as The Midnight Chime of Wishes. Legend has it on every Christmas Eve at precisely midnight. This bell would ring with a magical chime. And could grant a single whispered wish to one lucky soul…"

The room once more faded into darkness. Lily and Sophie now stood in the village square, surrounded by villagers from days long past. The villagers were wrapped in thick coats and scarves, their collective warm breath fogging in the chilly air. An ancient bell perched atop a tower stood silent, awaiting its moment to chime.

"Can you believe this, Lily?" Sophie whispered, her eyes alight with excitement. "We're actually here, on the night of the Midnight Chime! this book is amazing."

Lily, equally thrilled, nodded. "I wonder whose wish will be granted tonight."

With beaming faces, the villagers gathered around the bell. Their faces were lit with a mix of hope and anticipation, their eyes all fixed on the towering bell. Among the crowd, an elderly man with a gentle smile and a young girl holding her mother's hand caught Lily and Sophie's attention.

Sophie leaned towards the old man. "Have you been here before for the Midnight Chime?" she asked curiously.

"Oh, yes," he replied, his voice was soft and gentle. "Many years now. Each year, I come with a wish, but the joy for me is in the hoping, the dreaming. It's a night of magic, regardless of the wish."

Lily, moved by his words, smiled. As midnight approached, the excitement in the square was noticeable. The villagers fell silent, their eyes fixed on the bell tower. The air was filled with a tangible sense of wonder.

Sophie, her heart beating fast, whispered to Lily, "It's almost time. I wonder whose wish will come true. Do you think we are allowed to make a wish?"

"I don't see why not. We can try."

The clock struck the midnight hour, and on the last stroke, the bell began to chime. Its sound was clear and beautiful, resonating through the cold night air. The villagers closed their eyes, each silently whispering their wish.

As the final chime echoed, the young girl near Lily and Sophie opened her eyes, a bright smile spreading across her face. The villagers cheered, their voices filled with happiness and celebration.

Sophie turned to the girl. "Did you make a wish?"

The girl nodded, her eyes sparkling. "Yes, I wished for my mummy to be happy. She works so hard. I just want her to be happy and smile more."

Lily, touched by the girl's selflessness, said, "That's a beautiful wish. And it's already coming true." She pointed to the girl's mother, who was now smiling warmly at her daughter.

The old man, witnessing this exchange, chuckled softly. "See, the magic of the Midnight Chime is not just in the wishing, but in the love and joy it brings to us all."

As the celebration continued, Lily and Sophie felt a warmth in their hearts. They had experienced the magic of the Midnight Chime, a magic that was about more than just wishes; it was about hope, love, and the joy of Christmas.

Eventually, the world around them swirled once more, and they found themselves back in the Athenaeum, the book open before them.

"That was incredible," Sophie said, still feeling the magic of the moment. "The Midnight Chime of Wishes... it's about so much more than getting what you wish for."

Lily nodded in agreement. In the twinkling of an eye, a tiny figure appeared next to Lily, as if summoned by magic. It was Jingles, the Christmas elf, with a mischievous grin and eyes which sparkled like stars.

Sophie's eyes widened in amazement. "I can see him, Lily! I can really see Jingles!" she exclaimed, her voice bubbling with excitement.

Lily, with a warm smile, greeted their newfound friend. "Hello, Jingles."

Sophie, still in shock, turned to Jingles with curiosity. "So, this is what you look like! But how come I can see you now?"

Jingles chuckled, his laugh sounding like the jingle of tiny bells. "Ah, Sophie, it's because you've found the Christmas spirit in your heart. That's when true magic becomes visible. Have you both enjoyed your adventures in the book?"

Both girls replied in unison, their voices harmonising with excitement, "Oh yes!"

"It's been absolutely magical!" Sophie added, her face glowing with happiness and wonder.

Lily, her mind buzzing with thoughts, turned to Jingles with a question. "Jingles, are we allowed to take this magical book home with us?"

Jingles shook his head gently, his tiny hat wobbling. "No, not this book. It's special and must stay here in this room. But," he added with a twinkle in his eye, "You can take home the book with the secret keyhole. Just remember to sign it out first!"

Sophie and Lily nodded, understanding the importance of the rules in the library. They were grateful for the chance to bring a piece of the magic home with them.

As they prepared to leave, with the book safely signed out, Lily looked at Jingles. "Thank you for the magic, Jingles."

"And for letting us see you," Sophie added, her heart full of joy.

Jingles, with a final mischievous grin, disappeared in a flash of light, leaving behind a sprinkle of sparkling dust.

The girls, clutching the book with the secret keyhole, left the library. Their hearts and imaginations filled with the wonders they experienced. They knew every time they opened the book, they would be reminded of the magic of Christmas.

Moved by the poignant story of Oliver, Lily, and Sophie were determined to find his final resting place. Fuelled by a mix of curiosity and compassion, they embarked on their next quest with a sense of purpose. If they could locate Oliver's grave, they would speak with Sophie's mother and Mrs James, who were both well-respected in the community and ask them to help in reviving the forgotten tradition of honouring Oliver.

With a mix of excitement and solemnity, Lily and Sophie ventured to the cemetery, a serene place where time seemed to stand still. The cemetery, with its ancient headstones and moss-covered statues, had a tranquil yet melancholic air. They wandered among the graves, reading inscriptions faded by time, searching for any sign of Oliver.

Lily and Sophie trudged through the snow-blanketed cemetery, their eyes carefully scanning each gravestone. Some, mere mounds under the pristine white snow. The winter sun cast long, pale shadows across the snow, creating a serene yet sombre atmosphere for their quest.

"This is like a treasure hunt, but so much more meaningful," Lily whispered, her voice a blend of awe and seriousness, unusual for someone her age.

Sophie nodded, brushing snow off a nearby headstone. "Exactly. But how will we recognise Oliver's grave? Many of these stones are so weathered; the words are hard to read."

They made their way to a secluded corner of the cemetery, where ivy and snow clung to forgotten graves. Sophie stopped in front of a particularly worn gravestone, almost hidden under a thick layer of snow and ivy. "Look at this one," she said, her voice muffled by the cold air.

Together, they carefully brushed away the snow and ivy, revealing the faint outlines of letters on the gravestone. The stone felt icy and rough under their gloves, and the inscription was nearly erased by time and weather.

"Can you see anything?" Lily asked, her brow furrowed as she tried to decipher the faint letters.

Sophie removed a glove and traced her fingers along the shallow engravings, replied hesitantly, "I'm not sure... But there's an 'O' here, and maybe an 'L' over there. Look, here's a 'V'."

They continued in silence, gently uncovering more letters. "This is it, Lily," Sophie finally said, a note of certainty in her voice. "It just feels right, doesn't it?"

70

Lily stepped back, her eyes glistening with unshed tears of joy. "Yes, it does."

Sophie nodded, her expression thoughtful and caring. "We found you, Oliver. You will be remembered again."

They stood in silent tribute, paying their respects to a boy whose life, though they had never met, had touched theirs. The gentle rustle of the winter breeze through the bare branches seemed like a quiet acknowledgment of their discovery.

"We need to tell your mum and Mrs James about this," Lily said, breaking the silence. "They should know how to help us. We have to plan a service. Oliver deserves to be remembered."

Sophie's voice was firm with determination. "Absolutely. We'll make sure everyone in the Village hears about Oliver's story. This Christmas, his memory will be brought back to life."

With a renewed sense of purpose, Lily, and Sophie left the cemetery, inspired by their mission to revive Oliver's memory and rekindle a lost tradition in their village.

Sophie turned to Lily, "My mum will be at the tearooms with Mrs James, we should go there."

Lily and Sophie ran to the tearooms, their cheeks rosy from the cold and their hearts bursting with excitement. They entered the warm, cosy kitchen of the local tearoom. The delightful scent of freshly baked cookies permeated the air, making them feel a little peckish.

"Mum, Mrs James, we have something important to tell you," Sophie started, her voice rising eager to be heard.

Mrs James paused and turned towards the girls with a welcoming smile. "What is it, dear?" asked Sophie's mum.

Sophie's mum, comfortably seated at the kitchen table with a cup of tea, looked up with a spark of curiosity. "You girls seem quite excited. What's going on?"

Exchanging a quick, confirming look, Lily took a deep breath. "Well, we went to the cemetery today, searching for Oliver's grave. He's the boy from the story the Christmas tree told us. Oh! erm, we'll explain that part later."

Sophie picked up the narrative. "We think we found his grave. It's hidden away in a neglected part of the graveyard, covered in snow and overgrown with ivy."

Mrs James, her interest whetted, gestured for them to slow down. "Hold on a minute. Who is this Oliver you're talking about?"

Sophie then carefully recounted the heart-wrenching tale of Oliver, the young boy who tragically died trying to sell mistletoe in their village. She spoke of the village's initial outpouring of grief and the tradition of remembrance that followed, but has since been forgotten.

As Sophie narrated, her mother and Mrs James listened intently, their expressions turning from curiosity to a deep, reflective sadness. The story of Oliver, once a vivid chapter in the village's history, now seemed like a distant memory, lost in the passage of time.

Sophie's mother, visibly moved, spoke first. "I heard whispers of this story when I was a child, but I never knew the full details. It's heart-breaking."

Mrs James, a long-time resident of the village, nodded in agreement. "I remember my grandparents mentioning Oliver, but I'm sad to say that I, too, forgot the story. It's a shame we have let his memory fade away."

Sophie, with determination in her eyes, said, "That's why we want to do something. We want to revive the tradition of remembering Oliver. It's important, especially now during Christmas, when the village let him die."

Lily added, "We were thinking of organising a small service at his grave on Christmas Eve, like they used to do. We could start making it a tradition again, to remind us all of the spirit of the season and to remember who he was."

Sophie's mother, inspired by the girls' initiative, stood up decisively. "I think it's a wonderful idea. We should bring this tradition back. People like that deserve to be remembered. I'll help in any way I can."

Mrs James, always a community leader, agreed enthusiastically. "Let's do it. We can involve the church, the school, and the entire village. It'll be a beautiful way not just to honour Oliver but to bring the community together."

Plans began to take shape in the warm kitchen, as they discussed the logistics, from inviting the local vicar to organising volunteers. They spread the word through the village, using social media and at the village meeting to ensure a good turnout for the service.

Sophie's mother suggested, "We could also have a small fundraiser to help any families in need during this time of year, in Oliver's memory."

Mrs James smiled. "That's a splendid idea. It ties in perfectly with the spirit of giving and remembering the less fortunate."

Word of their initiative spread quickly through the village, rekindling interest in the forgotten story of the young, unfortunate mistletoe seller. The villagers, moved by the children's efforts, came together to clean and restore Oliver's grave. A small plaque was commissioned, bearing Oliver's name and a brief account of his story, ensuring his memory would never fade and be forgotten again.

Lily and Sophie, their hearts brimming with a sense of achievement, sat cross-legged on the plush carpet of Lily's bedroom, a haven of warmth and comfort. The soft glow of a bedside lamp cast a cosy light around them, heightening their sense of anticipation.

"I can't believe we actually did it, Lily!" Sophie exclaimed, her eyes sparkling with excitement. "What do you think our next adventure will be?"

Lily, her fingers gently traced the intricate cover of their secret book, replied with a determined smile, "We're going to bring the village of Santclausby back to life. It deserves its magic again."

Nodding in agreement, Sophie carefully inserted the key into the spine of the magic book. A moment later, a warm, yellowy light burst forth, enveloping them in its embrace. The familiar sensation of being transported swirled around them, and in a blink, they found themselves in the Athenaeum. The large book was already open on the central table as if expecting their arrival.

"The Winter Garden of Lights," Lily read aloud, from the title of the open chapter. Her voice echoed slightly in the bare space, adding to the sense of mystery.

As Sophie read the story, a magical light, softer and more inviting than before, engulfed them, whisking them away into the heart of the story.

Lily and Sophie stood in silent wonder as they watched the villagers of Santclausby busily create a magical garden under the early evening sky. The crisp winter air was filled with a sense of purpose and joy, as each villager, both young and old, contributed to the enchanting display.

The garden was a kaleidoscope of light, with lanterns of all shapes and sizes hanging from the bare branches of trees and placed carefully along the winding paths. Candles flickered behind ice-sculptures casting a ghostly glow on the surrounding snow. The effect was like stepping into a dream, a world where light and shadow danced gracefully.

"Look at this, Sophie," Lily whispered, pointing to a particularly intricate lantern, its light flickering gently. "This looks like the lantern we found, the magic lantern."

Sophie, her eyes reflecting the myriad of lights, nodded in agreement. "It does look like it, and there are ice carvings too. It seems to have its special place here in the middle of the display. I wonder why it's here?"

As they moved closer, they noticed the villagers gathering around the lantern, their faces illuminated by its soft glow. One by one, they began to make their wishes, speaking them softly as if sharing a precious secret with the night.

A young girl, no more than six, stepped forward, her small hand clutching a piece of paper. With a little help from her mother, she placed the paper inside the lantern, and they watched as it burnt, its ashes carried high on the breeze. "I wish for a puppy," the girl said shyly, her voice barely above a whisper.

An elderly man followed, his steps slow but steady. He took a moment to catch his breath before speaking his wish into the lantern. "I wish for health and happiness for my family," he said, his voice cracking with emotion.

Lily and Sophie watched, their hearts touched by the sincerity and simplicity of all the wishes. They could feel the hope and dreams of the villagers, each wish adding to the magic of the occasion.

As the night progressed, more villagers came, each adding their wish to the lantern. The garden became a living tribute to the community's hopes and dreams, a place where even the most hidden desires were given a voice.

Sophie turned to Lily, her eyes sparkling with an idea. "What if we make a wish, too? Maybe it will help bring back magic to the village."

Lily nodded, her eyes bright with excitement. "Let's do it. Let's see what happens."

They each took a piece of paper and wrote down their wishes. Lily wanted the village to come together and be happy again, while Sophie wanted the garden's magic to be part of their renewed traditions.

As they placed their wishes in the lantern, they felt a warm surge of hope, a feeling they were part of something special, a journey to rediscover its magic.

The night wore on, and the garden continued to glow with the light of a hundred wishes. The air was filled with a sense of peace and contentment, as if the garden itself was absorbing the hopes, dreams, and wishes of the villagers.

Lily and Sophie wandered through the garden. Each lantern and candle telling a story, each flickering light a reminder of the village's rich history and the bonds which once held it together.

The scene shimmered and faded; they were once more sitting the bedroom, the book now closed on the table before them.

The idea of resurrecting the tradition of the Winter Garden of Lights sparked a flame of hope in Lily and Sophie's hearts. As they sat in Lily's bedroom, surrounded by the gentle glow of fairy lights, Sophie's face lit up with a sudden inspiration. "Mum mentioned there's a Christmas meeting in the village hall tonight. That's our chance to share our idea!"

Lily's eyes shone with determination. "Yes, we need to get the village to do this again. It could really bring the village back together. We could make this a Christmas to remember."

Later that night, Lily, and Sophie, wrapped in their warmest coats, trudged through the snow-laden streets of their village. The melting snow squelching under their boots, a stark contrast to the flurry of thoughts and plans swirling in their minds. Their breath formed little clouds in the chilly air, each puff evidence of their nervous anticipation.

The village hall, usually a beacon of warmth and community, now stood stark and sombre under the harsh glare of fluorescent lights. Inside, villagers sat in disarray. Their faces etched with worry and doubt, mirroring the uncertainty about the future of their beloved village.

Sophie, summoning her courage, stepped forward, her small but clear voice slicing through the low hum of conversation. "Excuse me!" She exclaimed loudly, "Excuse me!"

The crowd slowly stopped chatting amongst themselves and looked straight at Sophie. Nervously, she started to speak. "We have an idea to bring back the village's Christmas spirit," she announced, scanning the crowd for a hint of support or interest.

Lily standing next to her chipped in, "We think reviving the Winter Garden of Lights could unite the village again, and bring in visitors from other towns and villages" she added, her voice slightly trembling but underscored with determination.

A voice from the crowd, dripping with incredulity, rang out, "And who gave you this idea?"

Exchanging a determined glance, Sophie replied, "It was Jingles, the Christmas elf..." A wave of laughter and mockery interrupted her as it swept through the hall. The villagers' disbelief was unmistakable.

Lily pressed on, her voice unwavering, "Jingles is not just a figment of our imagination. He's a magical being who has been part of some incredible adventures with us."

Their earnest words were met with jeers and sniggering. "Elves and magic? Are we in a children's fairy-tale?" someone shouted, their voice laced with scorn.

Undeterred, Sophie continued, "It was Jingles who showed us how to enter the Athenaeum, a realm of forgotten stories. He's been teaching us about the true spirit of Christmas."

The girls recounted their magical friend Jingles, speaking of his merry laugh and twinkling eyes, and the wonders of Christmas magic they had witnessed.

"He taught us the magic of Christmas lies in our hearts and in the joy we bring to others," Lily added, her voice heavy with emotion.

The hall erupted in a chorus of boos and hisses. The villagers' disbelief transforming into mocking laughter. "A Christmas elf and two little girls. How's this going to save our village? What nonsense! Go home and let the grown-ups get on with the meeting." Someone yelled.

"We've seen the magic. It's all true." Sophie concluded, her voice wavering under the weight of the mockery, "And we can bring it back to our village. The Winter Garden of Lights is more than just a display; it's a symbol of our unity and the joy we can share."

But the cacophony of laughter and scornful remarks drowned out their heartfelt plea out. "Children's fantasies won't save our village," another villager scoffed, the laughter growing louder.

Lily and Sophie stood amidst the scorn, their dream to rekindle the village's spirit crumbling before their eyes. The laughter and mocking voices echoed in their ears. A harsh reminder of the chasm between their magical world and the disbelieving reality of the villagers.

Defeated, and in floods of tears, they retreated and left the hall, the weight of rejection heavy on their young shoulders. Outside, the cold night air felt even more bitter, as if echoing the chill of disappointment gripping their hearts. The festive lights that once seemed magical now flickered mockingly, a stark reminder of their failure to convince the villagers.

As they made their way home, the laughter of the villagers haunted them, a cruel echo in the quiet, snowy streets. Their hope of uniting the village under the spell of Christmas magic had turned them into a laughingstock.

"I thought they would listen... I thought they would understand," Sophie sobbed, her voice barely above a whisper.

"We just wanted to help," Lily replied, her words heavy with disappointment. "But they couldn't see past their own disbelief."

The silence which followed was filled with a heavy sense of defeat. The magic and wonder they had experienced in the Winter Garden of Lights felt like a distant dream, one which the villagers were unwilling to embrace.

As they reached Lily's house, the warmth of the living room offered little comfort. The girls sat in silence, each lost in her own thoughts, the weight of the villagers' rejection pressing down on them.

But amidst the disappointment, a spark of determination flickered within them. They knew the magic they witnessed was real, and the potential it had to bring the village together was too important to give up on.

Lily, brushing a tear away and with her voice regaining strength, said, "Their disbelief won't stop us." "We know the magic of the Winter Garden of Lights is real. We just have to find another way to show them."

Chapter 7

It was mid-morning as Sophie and Lily trudged through the snow-laden streets of the village looking for inspiration and hoping Jingles would appear. Their boots crunching softly on the fresh snow underfoot. They couldn't forget the embarrassment and ridicule they had faced at last night's village meeting. Their cheeks, flushed from the cold, still burned with the sting of humiliation.

"Why did we even say anything?" Lily's voice was a whisper, lost in the muffling snow.

Sophie sighed, "I thought they'd believe us, Lily. I really did." Sophie's breath formed small clouds in the cold air as she turned to Lily, her voice tinged with the hurt she was trying to mask. "I still can't shake off how they laughed at us last night at the meeting, Lily. It was so... embarrassing."

Lily, pulling her coat tighter around her, looked down at the snow, her voice reflecting the wound to her pride. "Yeah, I thought they would at least listen to us. But all they did was laugh at us."

There was a pause, filled only by the soft crunch of their boots on the snow. Sophie, trying to find the right words, finally broke the silence. "But you know, Lily, we know what we saw. Jingles is real. They just don't believe because they can't see him like we can."

Lily glanced at Sophie, her eyes betraying a flicker of doubt. "Sometimes I wish I could just make them see, make them believe. It's hard when it feels like everyone is against you."

Sophie reached out, placing a comforting hand on Lily's shoulder. "I know, but we can't let them make us doubt ourselves. Remember what Jingles said about the magic of Christmas? It's about believing, even when no one else does. I didn't believe, but I do now. You brought my belief back Lily."

A small smile formed on Lily's face, her resolve strengthening. "You're right. We can't give up, especially not now. Jingles needs us. We have to be strong for him and for the magic of Christmas."

Sophie nodded, her own spirit bolstered by Lily's growing determination. "Exactly! We're in this together. We'll find a way to show them all that Christmas magic is real. The key is to persist and keep trying."

Lily's smile grew, and she looked at Sophie with gratitude. "Thanks, Sophie. I don't know what I'd do without you."

Sophie grinned, her own confidence now restored. "And your courage gives me hope. Let's not let what happened last night bring us down. We've got a mission to complete, and together, we can do anything."

As they continued their walk through the village, the memory of the previous night's humiliation still lingered, but it was now tempered by their shared resolve and the comfort of their unshakable bond.

As they passed the village square, a couple of older children, Jack, and Emma, spotted them. Jack, a tall boy with a mischievous glint in his eye, nudged Emma and smirked. "Hey, look who it is," he called out, loud enough for nearby villagers to hear.

Sophie's heart sank. She knew that tone all too well.

Emma, with her braids swinging, joined in, her voice laced with mock surprise. "Oh, it's the elf whisperers!"

The words hit Sophie and Lily like icy daggers. They quickened their pace, but Jack and Emma followed, their laughter echoing through the crisp morning air.

"Seen any elves lately?" Jack taunted, his boots sliding in the snow as he kept pace with them.

Emma chimed in, her voice dripping with sarcasm. "Oh look, it's the two who talk to a magic elf. Where's your magic elf now?"

Sophie felt a lump forming in her throat. She glanced at Lily, whose eyes were brimming with tears. The hurt in her friend's eyes was more painful than any taunt.

"Leave us alone," Sophie's voice was barely audible, a mix of anger and embarrassment.

Jack, undeterred, leaned in closer. "What's the matter? Cat got your tongue, or was it the elf?"

Emma laughed, a high-pitched, grating sound which seemed to fill the entire square. "Maybe their elf is on holiday. Too bad he didn't teach them any spells to make us disappear."

Invisible to the eyes of Jack and Emma, Jingles materialised next to Lily and Sophie. With a twinkling giggle, he nodded at the girls, acknowledging their distress. Before Jack and Emma could utter another taunt, Jingles swiftly enacted his playful retribution. A subtle flick of his fingers a patch of snow beneath the bullies' feet turned as slick as glass. And with a comical lack of grace, they slipped and tumbled into a heap of flailing limbs and shocked expressions. The snow muffled the sound of their fall, but the girls' laughter rang clear and bright against the winter air.

"Why can't you leave us alone?" scolded Sophie, her voice firm yet tinged with an edge of amusement as she watched the spectacle unfold. Jack, dishevelled and bewildered, his usual bravado faltering as he attempted to regain his footing. "Make your elf appear then!" he challenged, brushing snow from his clothes, oblivious to the invisible orchestrator of his fall.

"Leave us alone, or you'll be sorry." Lily's voice, quivering slightly with emotion, cut through the cold air. She took a step forward, her stance small but unmistakably defiant. "You're just being mean, and mean people come off worse."

Emma, attempting to salvage some dignity, rolled her eyes and scoffed, "Oh, come on, they're not worth it. Everyone knows elves aren't real." Unseen by the bullies, Jingles danced around them, his movements quick and light. He jumped up and tapped Jack's shoulder with some force, sending him spinning in a confused circle. Emma found herself being pushed back into the pile of snow by an invisible hand. The girls, their faces now lighting up with glee, stood at a safe distance, watching as Jingles executed his playful mischief on the unsuspecting bullies. Each trick, unseen but the effects were clear, each one more amusing and clever than the last, bringing a sense of poetic justice to the scene.

Jingles, with his elfish agility, subtly untied Jack's shoelaces. As Jack strutted about, trying to maintain an air of arrogance, he trod on his shoelace and stumbled. The girls stifled their giggles behind their hands, exchanging looks of delight. Next, while Jack's misfortune distracted Emma, Jingles swiftly moved behind her. He carefully placed another small, slippery patch of ice right where she was standing. As she attempted to walk, she found herself once again slipping and sliding comically, struggling to keep her balance. The girls couldn't help but laugh openly now.

Then, Jack and Emma made some large snowballs, which they intended to throw at Lily and Sophie. With a flick of his elfin magic, he transformed the snowballs into harmless, fluffy piles of snow. When the bullies attempted to throw them, they poofed into powdery clouds. The bullies were left looking bewildered and covered in snow.

The air filled with laughter and powdered snow. Jack and Emma were no longer the menacing figures from moments before. Rather, two children caught up in a bizarre, inexplicable series of misadventures. Emma, her braids now appeared to dance as though they had a mind of their own. "Stop this!" she cried. "Despite their best efforts to stay gruff, Lily and Sophie's infectious laughter broke through their tough facade. Finally, Jingles, pleased with the morning's adventures, nodded to the girls and vanished with a sparkling wink, as quietly as he came."

The girls watched all these happenings with a mixture of amusement and satisfaction. Jingles' tricks were harmless, yet effective in teaching the bullies a lesson about kindness and respect. Jingles had managed to turn the tables on the bullies without harm, using his magic to create a scene filled with laughter and light-heartedness. As the tormentors retreated, defeated and confused, Lily and Sophie shared a high-five, their spirits lifted by the sight of justice served in such a uniquely magical way. Jingles' playful antics had done more than protect Lily and Sophie; they turned a tough day into one of joy and triumph. His clever tricks whilst outsmarting the bullies also filled the girls' hearts with glee. Sophie looked around. A few villagers had stopped to watch the spectacle, their expressions a mix of curiosity and amusement. Sophie felt a surge of defiance. "You may not believe in elves, but that doesn't justify you mocking our belief," she said, her voice now filled with strength. "The village of Santclausby is supposed to be about magic and belief. Or have you forgotten that?"

Jack's smirk faded slightly, replaced by a flicker of uncertainty. Emma, too, seemed taken aback by Sophie's words. Sophie continued, her voice steady. "We saw an elf, or we didn't. That's our belief, and it's not for you to mock."

There was a moment of silence, the only sound being the gentle rustle of the wind through the bare branches of the trees.

Finally, Jack shrugged, his bravado seeming to wane. Emma nudged him, and they turned to leave, their laughter no longer as loud or confident.

Sophie and Lily watched them go, a sense of relief washing over them. They exchanged a meaningful glance, silently promising to remain steadfast in their beliefs and spirit, especially with Jingles as their guardian.

As they walked away, an elderly man with a gentle demeanour approached them. His eyes were kind, and his voice carried the softness of someone who had lived many a winter. "Are you two alright?" he asked, his tone infused with genuine concern. "I saw those other children taunting you. Luckily, they went away before I got here. Otherwise, they would have got a piece of my mind."

Lily, caught slightly off guard, replied with a hint of briskness in her voice, "Yes, we're fine."

The old man nodded, a wise smile playing on his lips. "Well, I just thought you needed to know, I believe you. You are right, you know; this village needs to return to its roots. We should bring back the old values, re-embrace the Christmas spirit of the past, and remind the people of how this village came to be."

Lily's expression softened, curiosity replacing her initial defensiveness. "What do you mean?" she inquired.

The man leaned on his cane, his eyes reflecting the twinkling lights around them. "This village was once a beacon of the Christmas spirit, a place where joy, generosity, and community thrived. But over the years, we've lost a lot of that. It's time we remembered what made this village special."

Lily's, her eyes wide with intrigue, added, "That sounds wonderful. But how can we help bring it back? People don't believe us; they think we are making it all up."

The old man looked at both girls, a spark of hope in his eyes. "By sharing stories, reviving traditions, and showing everyone the true meaning of Christmas, you can get this community to come together. Don't stop at each obstacle in your way. Examine other methods to navigate around them. Ah, the book from the Athenaeum is indeed a fascinating book," he remarked, his voice trailing off as he sauntered away.

Lily and Sophie exchanged startled glances, both surprised he knew about their special book and its origin. They turned back to where the old man had stood, but he was nowhere to be seen.

"Where did he go?" Sophie asked in bewilderment.

Lily, still scanning the area for any sign of the old man, shook her head in disbelief. "It's like he was a part of the magic we've been reading about. It's possible he was more than just an old man, could he have been Santa in disguise?"

"How did he know about the book?"

Lily shrugged, "I have no idea."

The mystery deepened as the soft glow of the streetlamps cast a gentle warm light on the snow-laden paths.

"He could have been part of the book." Sophie suggested.

Lily looked puzzled at Sophie's response. "What do you mean?"

"Well, we visited those places in the storybook. It might be possible the people from those stories can visit us."

Lily, her mind racing with possibilities, nodded. "Maybe you're right. We can help revive the Christmas spirit here."

Sophie's eyes sparkled with excitement. "Yes! And we can start with the Winter Garden of Lights."

"I have an idea that just might work. Is it possible Mrs James would lend us her lantern. We should speak to her.

The girls, their spirits lifted by a newfound purpose, made their way through the village. Their footsteps leaving a trail of hope behind them. They talked about their plans, their voices filled with a stout conviction. Sophie, her heart aglow with anticipation, agreed wholeheartedly. "This is going to be amazing, Lily. We're going to bring the Christmas spirit back to this village!"

Sophie paused outside Mrs James' tearoom, captivated by the festive lights and wreath. "Do you think she'll lend us the lantern? What if she's worried about what the villagers might say?"

Lily, her resolve as strong as ever, replied confidently, "She's seen the magic of the lantern before, just like your mum did. We need to show more people the magic. Once they see it, they'll understand, and they'll be on our side."

Sophie nodded, drawing strength from Lily's conviction. She pushed open the door to the tearoom, where as always the warmth enveloped them. Mrs James looked up from her counter.

"Ah, Lily and Sophie! What brings you here on such a cold day?" Mrs James inquired, her eyes twinkling like the fairy lights gracing her tearoom.

"I suppose you heard about last night?" Lily whispered.

"I did. The village should be ashamed of itself. Come on, come round the back." She beckoned, "Right, what can I do for you two?"

Sophie took a deep breath, her words laced with hope. "Mrs James, we need your help. We're planning something special to bring back the Christmas spirit to the village, and to prove the village has magic."

Mrs James, intrigued, leaned forward. "Oh? And how can I assist in this wonderful endeavour?"

Lily, her eyes shining with excitement, explained. "We want to organise a Winter Garden of Lights, like the village did all those years ago. We could use your lantern to start the magic. It could be a night where the entire village comes together, sharing stories and traditions, just like in the old days."

Mrs James' face lit up with understanding and delight. "What a splendid idea! The lantern is yours to use. If it was not for you two finding it in the first place, I would not have it now. I've always believed in the magic of Christmas, and it's high time we shared that with everyone."

Sophie's relief was evident, and she beamed with gratitude. "Thank you, Mrs James! Thank you. With your lantern, we can show everyone the magic they've been missing."

"Is there anything I can help with preparing for the Winter Garden of Lights? My back garden is large, but I fear not large enough to accommodate the village."

Lily spoke up. "Where do you suggest we could do it?"

"Let's think about it overnight. Come and see me tomorrow and we will speak again."

The two girls thanked Mrs James and left with the lantern as promised to them. Sophie and Lily left the tearoom, their hearts filled with a sense of purpose and joy. The old man's mystery and their magical book adventures had ignited a flame in Sophie and Lily. They were determined to spread this flame throughout the village. Walking back along the main road, they were lost in their plans and dreams. Around them, the air seemed charged with the possibility of rekindling the village's Christmas spirit. As they moved, an unseen thread of magic seemed to weave through their hearts, stretching out to touch the very soul of the village.

Lily and Sophie walked through the village streets, their minds buzzing with ideas and plans for the Winter Garden of Lights. The golden glow from the windows of the houses cast a warm, inviting light on their path, giving them a cosy feeling inside.

"Where could we have it?" Sophie pondered aloud it needs to be somewhere big enough for everyone.

Lily, her scarf wrapped snugly around her neck, nodded thoughtfully, "Mrs James will think of somewhere good."

As they walked, they passed the village park, its bare trees standing like silent sentinels in the soft glow of the moonlight. A sudden realisation dawned on Lily. "What about the park? With some lights, decorations, and Mrs James' lantern, it could be transformed into a winter wonderland!"

Sophie's eyes lit up with excitement. "That's perfect, Lily! We can hang lanterns from the trees, and along the path. And if we light Mrs James' lantern last, hopefully it will be as magical as in her garden."

The girls' conversation was filled with enthusiasm as they envisioned their plan coming to life.

As they arrived at the park, they paused to observe their surroundings. "In their minds, they saw the park lit up. Echoing with villagers' laughter and chatter, feeling the community's warmth finally come together."

"Will we need to talk to the village council to get permission?" Lily asked.

"No, they will just mock us again. We need to hear what Mrs James comes up with. She may know who would help us, too."

They headed off home, eager to know what tomorrow would bring.

"Sophie, I just had a great idea. Let's open the magic book and read the Winter Garden of Lights again. That way, we can take notes on how to recreate it, you know, like they did all those years ago."

Sophie's face and eyes lit up as she nodded in agreement. Lily and Sophie, their hearts pulsing with excitement and curiosity, ran all the way back to Lily's house. They ran straight upstairs and pulled the magic book from the shelf in her bedroom. Sophie inserted the key into its spine. In a flash of twinkling light, they found themselves back in the Athenaeum. Sitting at the table, Lily opened the ancient book. Turning the pages, Lily stopped and looked at Sophie and smiled.

"The Winter Garden of Lights," Lily read aloud, her voice echoing a sense of achievement. As she started to read, eager to revisit the story, a cascade of warm magical light enveloped them, transporting them once again into the very heart of the tale.

They found themselves in a vast, enchanting space, far more grandiose than the cosy confines of Mrs James' garden at the rear of the tea rooms. This was a world where fantasy blended seamlessly with reality. The villagers, moving with purpose and joy, were in the midst of transforming their surroundings into the fabled Winter Garden of Lights.

Sophie, in a hushed tone and filled with awe, remarked to Lily, "This is like Mrs James' garden, but bigger."

Lily, her enthusiasm dampened just for a moment, replied with a hint of disappointment, "You're right, Sophie. We can't do this in her garden. It won't be big enough."

Sophie, with reassuring confidence, added, "Perhaps the location isn't important. It might be magical wherever it's done."

The lanterns captured their attention, varying in shapes and sizes, adorning the bare branches and lining the serpentine path. Each lantern, with its own flickering candle, added an element of mystique and warmth to the winter night.

Sophie, her face etched with a tinge of concern, gestured towards the ice sculptures, intricately carved and gleaming in the lantern light of those placed behind them. "Those ice carvings are magnificent. But how can we possibly have those in our garden?"

Lily, her eyes reflecting the soft, golden hues of the lanterns, smiled reassuringly. "Remember, magic played a part here. When Mrs James lit her lantern, ice carvings appeared by magic. Maybe, just maybe, we'll be fortunate enough to witness the same again."

Sophie nodded, her spirits raised by the thought. "We'll still need a lot of candles and lanterns."

As they walked further, their eyes fell upon a lantern, shining brighter, its light more enchanting than the others. "There's Mrs James' lantern!" Lily pointed out excitedly. "It must be the source of those magical ice carvings."

Wandering through the garden, they observed villagers meticulously arranging lanterns, ensuring everywhere was bathed in a soft glow. They watched in fascination as the ice sculptures' surfaces sparkled like stars.

Sophie scribbled in her notebook, "We'll need strings of lights, and we can ask Mrs James to ask other villagers to contribute lanterns."

They spent the next few hours immersed in this magical world, absorbing every detail, every nuance of the Winter Garden of Lights. As darkness enveloped the sky, the garden burst into a spectacle of light and shadow, an exquisite spectacle which left them breathless.

"This is what we need to bring to our village," Sophie whispered, her eyes aglow with the reflected light of a thousand lanterns.

Lily nodded in agreement. "Our garden will be different, but it will be special in its own way. Even if it is only half as good as this, I will be proud of it."

As they prepared to leave, they took one last look at the Winter Garden of Lights, its beauty etched in their minds. The magic book, sensing their readiness, swirled its light around them, transporting them back to their world.

Back in the room, with the book closed before them, Lily and Sophie were filled with a newfound determination. They had witnessed the magic and now it was their turn to create an enchanting night of their own, filled with light and laughter.

With Mrs James' lantern promised to them, they set out to organise their version of the Winter Garden of Lights.

"Where's Jingles?" asked Lily. "We could do with his help."

Lily called out, "Jingles! We need your help."

Chapter 8

It was now December 22nd and Lily and Sophie were excited to go and see Mrs James. The girls, brimming with ideas and excitement, made their way to Mrs James' tearoom, where she greeted them with a smile.

"I have been talking with some friends of mine who are eager to help us with the Winter Garden of Lights," Mrs James announced, her enthusiasm infectious.

Sophie clapped her hands in delight. "That's wonderful! I hope we can get lots of people involved."

Lily's eyes sparkled with a sudden burst of inspiration, their depths catching the light like tiny stars against a night sky. "What if," she began, her voice bubbling with excitement, "We added a Starlight Procession to the event?"

Mrs. James leaned in closer. Her eyes shimmered with intrigue, and her warm, encouraging smile deepened the fine lines around her mouth, like a snowflake spreading its intricate patterns. "A Starlight Procession, you say? That does sound absolutely delightful. But tell me, what exactly would it entail?"

"Well," Lily began, her voice soft and dreamy, like she was telling the most magical secret, "people could sing Christmas carols while they walk through the streets, holding a lantern or a candle in their hands. It'd be so pretty, all those little lights shining in the dark, like stars we can carry. And when everyone reaches the Winter Garden, we could use all those lanterns and candles to light it up, turning it into the most beautiful place ever. It would look like a Christmas fairyland, all sparkly and glowing, like it's been sprinkled with stardust."

Her words painted a picture that seemed to hang in the air, like little puffs of breath on a chilly day. She imagined the village streets, usually just plain and normal, turning into a shining path full of light, with the lanterns flickering and making shadows that would dance on the snowy footpaths. "The smell of pine trees and warm, cider would mix with the cold, fresh air, and you'd hear the carollers singing, their voices bouncing off the old cobblestone walls. It would be like the lanterns weren't just glowing, they'd be carrying all the wishes and dreams of the people holding them, leading everyone right to the Winter Garden, where everything would sparkle and shine, like the magic was finally waking up." She continued.

Mrs. James could almost feel the warmth from the candles as she imagined it. Sophie, who had been quietly observing, let a soft smile spread across her face, her eyes crinkling at the corners as she nodded her approval. "Yes," she murmured, "I think that would be truly magical."

"It would certainly add to the festive atmosphere and increase the number of lanterns needed for the Winter Garden. It would make it even more special." Mrs James paused in thought, and then continued, "I could set up a hot chocolate stall. Everyone in the procession would get a free drink to warm them up in this chilly weather. That should encourage people to attend."

Sophie's eyes sparkled with gratitude. "That's so generous of you, Mrs James. It will definitely encourage more people to join the procession; your hot chocolate is world famous."

Mrs James chuckled, "I don't know about being world famous, but the people in the village seem to like it."

Lily's eyes sparkled with excitement. "We think it should start at the village church. It's such a beautiful starting point and the choir could lead the procession."

Sophie, standing beside her, nodded in agreement. "Yeah, and then we could wind our way through the main streets. It'd be like a twinkling path leading everyone right up to the Winter Garden of Lights."

Mrs James, a warm smile on her face, leaned on the counter of her quaint tea room. "That sounds lovely, girls. But have you thought about the route? We need to make sure it's not too long for the little ones, but still long enough to be special."

Lily rubbed her chin thoughtfully. "How about we go down Oak Street and then turn at the Market Square? That way, we can cover most of the village without making it too tiring."

Mrs James nodded approvingly. "Very smart thinking. And what about the lanterns? We must ensure they're safe, especially with so many children joining in."

Lily bounced on her toes, clearly excited. "We could use LED candles! They're safe and look just like real candles! Plus, everyone could decorate their own lanterns."

Sophie grinned. "The best part will be all of us walking together, lighting up the whole village!"

Mrs James looked at the two girls fondly. "You two have done a fantastic job planning this. The Starlight Procession will definitely be a highlight of the Winter Garden event. I'll speak to the other shopkeepers and get them involved too. It'll be a wonderful village effort."

"I'll talk to mum, see if she can get the local choir to help with the singing," Sophie suggested.

"And I'll see if we can get some lanterns and candles from people wanting to help," Lily added, already making a mental list of things to do.

As they left the tearoom, the cold winter air hit them, but it did nothing to dampen their spirits. The village, with its charming houses and festive decorations, was the ideal setting for their Starlight Procession and Winter Garden of Lights.

Lily and Sophie, fuelled by their boundless energy and excitement, became a whirlwind of activity throughout the village. With determination and a shared sense of purpose, they embarked on their mission to spread the word about the Starlight Procession and the enchanting Winter Garden of Lights. Their first task was creating the posters. They spent hours at Sophie's kitchen table, surrounded by an array of colourful markers, glitter pens, and stacks of paper. Each poster was crafted with care, their young hands diligently drawing festive motifs, twinkling stars, glowing lanterns, and the silhouettes of a merry procession. Bold letters, carefully outlined in glitter, invited the villagers to join in the magical evening.

Once the posters were ready, the girls set out to distribute them around the village. They started at the village square, at the community bulletin board. Carefully, they pinned up their bright, eye-catching posters, ensuring they were in prime positions for all to see. Their next stop was the village's quaint high street. Here, they visited each shop, from the cosy bakery with its mouth-watering aroma of freshly baked bread, to the small local bookshop. At each stop, they were met with smiles and words of encouragement from the shopkeepers, many of whom promised to attend and spread the word.

The girls made their way along the winding streets, stopping at key points where villagers often gathered. The post office, the library, and even the village hall. No spot was left without a poster. Their excitement was infectious, and soon they had enlisted the help of some of their friends, turning their duo into a small army of enthusiastic promoters.

By the end of the day, the news of the Starlight Procession had spread like wildfire. The posters, with their cheerful designs and inviting message, had captured the villagers' imagination. Lily and Sophie, tired but exhilarated from their day's work, stood in the village square as the sun began to set, looking at one of their posters fluttering gently in the breeze. They shared a smile, a silent acknowledgment of their successful mission. The village was set to come alive with the spirit of Christmas, and it was all thanks to their efforts and the charming allure of the Starlight Procession and the Winter Garden of Lights.

Sophie's mum had managed to enlist the local church choir, who were more than happy to lead the carol singing. Meanwhile, Lily went from door to door, speaking with the villagers and collecting spare lanterns and candles.

Later that day, Sophie, noticing that Lily hadn't been her usual lively self during the planning, decided to check in on her friend. She found Lily sitting quietly in her room, the sparkle that always lit up her eyes now dimmed by doubt and worry.

"Lily, why are you hiding away? What's the matter?" Sophie asked gently, her voice soft and filled with the kind of concern that only a true friend can offer.

Lily looked up, her voice barely more than a whisper. "I feel like I've let everyone down. We don't have enough lanterns or candles. How can we make the Winter Garden magical with so little?"

Without a moment's hesitation, Sophie sat on the bed beside her, wrapping an arm around Lily's shoulders and squeezing her close. "Do you remember the time I stopped believing in Santa? You were the one who brought that magic back to me, even when I thought it was gone forever. And since then, we've seen so many wonderful things happen, haven't we? You've always found a way to make things special."

"But what if this time, it's just not enough?" Lily's eyes were shiny as tears filled her eyes, her worry tugging at her heart.

Sophie took Lily's hands in her own, holding them tightly, as if to transfer every bit of warmth and love she had. "It will be enough, Lily. We'll take our eight lanterns and twelve candles and make them shine as brightly as a hundred, maybe even more. Because it's not about how many we have; it's about the magic we put into them. And with you leading us, I know we'll make something beautiful."

Lily felt a warmth spread through her chest, her fears melting away like snow touched by the morning sun.

Suddenly, there was a flash of light, and Jingles appeared. "Jingles, where have you been?" Lily asked, her tears momentarily forgotten.

"I've been around, watching," Jingles replied. "You've done more than you realise, Lily. We needed to see the strength of your belief in Christmas."

"But I... I haven't done anything. Everything feels like a failure," Lily sobbed, her tears resuming their path down her cheeks.

"You've done a lot," Jingles assured her. "You've turned doubters into believers. You found Mrs James' lantern. You also revived the story of Oliver and stirred excitement about old customs in the village."

Lily pondered his words. "Sophie helped too."

"Yes, she has," Jingles agreed. "And you both aren't finished yet. Someone special has sent you a gift. Put on your coats and head down to the park."

Filled with curiosity and a renewed sense of hope, Lily and Sophie hurried to the park. As they arrived, a breathtaking sight greeted them. The park, usually dark and quiet, was transformed. Lanterns, lots of lanterns, lit up the paths and trees. The park was alive with a soft, warm glow, turning it into a magical wonderland.

"Who did this?" Lily gasped, her eyes wide with wonder.

Jingles just smiled. "Now go and bring this village back to life."

Lily turned to thank Jingles, but he had vanished in his usual puff of sparkling smoke.

Mrs James arrived, pushing a cart filled with steaming hot chocolate and delicious treats. "I thought we might need a little extra warmth tonight," she said, her eyes twinkling.

As the evening of the Winter Garden of Lights unfolded, the village was enveloped in a sense of enchantment and anticipation. The event began at the village church, where the choir stood ready. Their voices ready to enliven the village with a medley of carols, cutting through the crisp winter air. The church, adorned with festive decorations, served as the perfect starting point for the Starlight Procession. Led by the local choir, a harmonious ensemble of voices from within the community, the Starlight Procession began its enchanting journey. The choir members, dressed in warm festive attire, their faces alight with joy, led the way, their voices rising in a beautiful rendition of classic Christmas carols. Behind them, villagers of all ages followed, forming a meandering river of light and sound through the heart of the village. Each villager held a candle encased in a glass wind protector or a lantern, which flickered and danced like tiny stars against the backdrop of the night sky. The candles, a myriad of tiny flames, creating a magical spectacle, illuminating the procession with a soft, golden glow. Children, their eyes wide with wonder, held their LED candles, mesmerised by the fake flames. Adults, smiling and singing, walked hand in hand or with arms around each other, basking in the communal warmth of the event.

As the procession moved, their voices joined with those of the choir, creating a symphony of joyous sound. The familiar melodies of Christmas carols, 'Silent Night', 'O Holy Night', and 'Deck the Halls', filled the air. Carols echoing off the buildings and enveloping the village in a musical embrace. The songs, sung with true heartfelt emotion, resonated with the spirit of the season, evoking memories and a sense of nostalgia among the participants. The glow from the candles cast a warm, enchanting light on the faces of the villagers, highlighting their expressions of joy, togetherness, and festive cheer. This light did more than just brighten their path; it reflected the inner glow of a community united in celebration and the spirit of the season. As the procession wound its way through the main streets, residents who weren't walking in it came out of their homes to watch. They stood in doorways and leaned out of windows, some joining in the singing, their voices adding to the growing chorus.

The procession made its way towards the entrance of the park; the anticipation growing as they neared the Winter Garden of Lights. Flickering candlelight, combined with the vibrant voices, created an atmosphere which was both uplifting and serene. It was a perfect prelude to the wonder that awaited them in the garden. As the villagers reached the entrance, the spectacular sight of the Winter Garden greeted them. Hundreds of twinkling lights adorned the trees and pathways, transforming the park into a winter wonderland. The contrast between the gentle candlelight and the vibrant garden lights was breath-taking, marking the culmination of a truly magical Starlight Procession. The villagers, now gathered in the park, and continued to sing, their voices a joyful celebration of the season.

At that moment, as if to add to the enchantment, it began to snow. Gentle flakes drifted down from the heavens, dusting the trees, and the hair of the villagers with a delicate layer of white. The snowflakes caught the light from the lanterns, creating a scene which was magical to behold.

Some villagers, who had not joined the procession, were already in the park, awaiting the arrival of the Starlight Procession. Their faces lit up with delight as they watched the procession enter the park, the choir's singing growing louder and more triumphant.

Mrs James, near her hot chocolate stall, clapped with delight. "Welcome, everyone, to the Winter Garden of Lights!" she announced, her voice filled with warmth. "Please, help yourselves to hot chocolate. Let's keep the cold at bay on this magical night."

The villagers gathered around her stall, their hands wrapped around steaming cups of hot chocolate warming their cold hands. Their faces aglow with the light of the lanterns and the joy of the moment. The children, their cheeks rosy from the cold, didn't seem to mind as they laughed and played their innocence, adding to the magic of the evening.

Sophie, looking around at the gathered crowd, leaned towards Lily. "Can you believe we made this happen? And it's all thanks to you."

Lily, her eyes shining with happiness and pride, replied, "It's more beautiful than I ever imagined. Look at everyone, Sophie. We did it. We did it together."

The choir continued to sing, their voices resonating throughout the park. The harmonies they created were a fitting soundtrack to the evening, a reminder of the enduring spirit of Christmas.

As the night progressed, villagers shared stories and sang along to the carols. The atmosphere was one of togetherness and joy, a demonstration of the power of community and the magic of believing.

Amid the celebration, Lily, and Sophie took a moment to step back and take it all in. They watched as the snowflakes gently fell, as the laughter and singing filled the air, and as the light from the lanterns and candles cast a warm, golden hue over everything. The Winter Garden of Lights was in full swing, its magic enveloping the whole park. Mrs James, holding a microphone, called for attention, her voice clear and warm against the backdrop of gentle conversations and laughter. "Ladies and gentlemen, boys, and girls, may I have your attention, please?"

The chatter subsided, and all eyes turned towards Mrs James, who stood beside the central lantern on its stone plinth. "I would like to take a moment to acknowledge the incredible young ladies who made this enchanting evening possible. Let's hear it for Lily and Sophie!"

The crowd erupted into applause, clapping enthusiastically for the two girls who had worked tirelessly to bring this magical event to life. Lily and Sophie, blushing with pride and a bit overwhelmed by the attention, stepped forward.

"And now," Mrs James continued, her eyes twinkling, "I invite Lily and Sophie to light our final lantern, the magical lantern which started it all."

Lily and Sophie, each holding a long candle taper, approached Mrs James' lantern. They stood by her side, their eyes reflecting the excitement and wonder of the moment. Mrs James lit their tapers and invited them to light the lantern, Lily, and Sophie together carefully lit the candle, and as they did, ice sculptures, intricate and shimmering, started to materialise throughout the park, sparkling like giant diamonds amongst the crowd. Their appearance added an ethereal quality to the already magical atmosphere. The sculptures, in various shapes and sizes, seemed to capture the very essence of winter's beauty.

The crowd gasped in astonishment, their cheers, and applause filling the air. "Wow, look at that!" exclaimed a young boy, pointing at a sculpture of a reindeer glistening under the lights.

"It's like a winter fairy tale come to life," murmured an elderly lady, her eyes misty with emotion.

Sophie, beaming with joy, turned to Lily. "Can you believe this? It's even more magical than we ever imagined."

Lily, her eyes wide with wonder, nodded. "It's like a dream. I never thought it would turn out this beautiful."

The children in the crowd, running from one sculpture to another, were particularly captivated, adding their laughter and excitement to the festive atmosphere. Parents followed, cameras in hand, capturing every joyous moment.

Mrs James, watching the scene with a contented smile, said to Lily and Sophie, "You two have brought so much joy to our village tonight. This is a night we will all remember for years to come."

The choir resumed their singing, their voices blending perfectly with the magical setting. Villagers joined in, singing along to familiar carols, their voices carrying through the crisp winter air.

Sophie and Lily, standing side by side, took a moment to soak in the scene. The park, illuminated by lanterns and the soft glow of the ice sculptures, was alive with the spirit of Christmas. People mingled and marvelled at the surrounding beauty.

As the evening progressed, Mrs James' hot chocolate proved to be a hit, with villagers queuing up for an extra cup of the steaming, rich drink. The laughter and chatter continued, the sense of community and togetherness unmistakable.

"This is what Christmas is about," Lily whispered to Sophie, her heart full. Lily nodded, her eyes shining with happiness. "We did it, Sophie. We really did it."

The Winter Garden of Lights turned into a celebration of community spirit, a night when the magic of Christmas was not just felt but seen and shared.

As the night drew to a close and the villagers made their way home, the atmosphere in the park was one of contentment and joy. The choir's final carol, a harmonious rendition of "Silent Night," lingered in the air, wrapping the evening in a blanket of tranquillity.

Lily and Sophie, standing arm in arm, surveyed the park, now muted and serene. The lanterns, their light dimming, still cast a gentle glow. The ice sculptures, though now just memories, had left an indelible mark on everyone's hearts.

"The Winter Garden of Lights was more than just an event; it was a magical experience, a cherished memory for our village," Lily said softly, her eyes reflecting the fading lights.

Sophie nodded in agreement. "It's evidence of what we can achieve when we believe and come together. The magic of community has truly come alive tonight."

Mrs James approached them, her face radiant with a broad, satisfied grin. "This rekindled tradition will endure for many years, all thanks to you two," she said, her eyes twinkling with pride.

Sophie's and Lily's parents came to take them home, their expressions a mix of admiration and pride. "We can't believe you two managed all of this," Lily's mum exclaimed, her voice filled with affection.

"We had a lot of help from Sophie's mum and Mrs James," Lily responded modestly.

"And Jingles," Sophie added with a smile.

Lily's mum looked puzzled. "Who's Jingles?"

The girls laughed in unison. "He's a magic Christmas elf," Lily explained, her eyes sparkling with mischief.

"Well, after tonight, I'm prepared to believe in all sorts of magic," Lily's mum said, her voice carrying a note of wonder.

Mrs James, holding her lantern, gave the girls a knowing smile and gently blew out the candle. As the flame flickered and died, the last vestiges of the ice sculptures vanished, leaving behind a sense of enchantment.

"There's a lot more magic in this village than people realise," Mrs James said thoughtfully. "And these two are reviving it, bringing it back to life for all of us to experience."

As they walked home, the gentle glow of the lanterns fading behind them, Lily and Sophie felt a deep sense of fulfilment. They had not only created a memorable event, but also reawakened the magic of Christmas in the hearts of their fellow villagers.

The Winter Garden of Lights would be remembered not just for its beauty and enchantment, but as the night when two young girls reminded everyone of the joy, wonder, and community spirit which lay at the heart of the festive season.

Chapter 9

The 23rd of December finally arrived, a day filled with anticipation and excitement for the girls. They were both in Lily's bedroom, their hearts fluttering like the wings of a butterfly in the summer. "What shall we do today?" asked Sophie.

"let's go and take a look in the park, see what it looks like in the daylight."

They wrapped up in their warm outdoor clothes and set off for the park. The village was alive with excitement. Everywhere Lily and Sophie went, they could hear the villagers talking about the magical evening they had experienced. The local bakery, the post office, even the streets were filled with the buzz of animated conversations and laughter.

"That was the best event the village has seen in years!" exclaimed Mrs Barker to Mr. Smith as they stood outside the bakery, the smell of fresh bread wafting through the air.

The girls, walked through the village, with a sense of pride and accomplishment. They exchanged smiles, their hearts swelling with joy at the impact of their efforts.

"I can't believe all these people are talking about it!" Sophie said, her eyes shining with delight.

Lily nodded in agreement.

"Hello, you two," said Mrs Roberts, "It's like you've brought a new spark back to the village. And those ice sculptures! I'm still trying to figure out how you did it."

Sophie giggled. "If only they knew about Mrs James' lantern and the magic which brought them to life!" She whispered to Lily.

As they continued their walk, they entered the park to see what it looked like in the daylight. The park, which had been the centre of magic and light the night before, lay quiet and serene under the soft glow of the morning sun, and a blanket of fresh snow.

Some lanterns were still hanging from the trees, their candles long since extinguished. The ice sculptures were gone, leaving behind only the memories of their sparkling beauty. The paths, once filled with laughter and the sound of carols, were now empty, but the magic of the previous night still lingered in the air.

Lily picked up a fallen lantern from the ground, her fingers tracing the delicate patterns on its surface. Sophie, looking around at the empty paths and quiet trees, added, "It's amazing how different it looks by day. But you can still feel the magic, can't you?"

Lily nodded as they walked through the park. They recounted their favourite moments from the Winter Garden of Lights.

"I think we've started something special, Lily. Reviving an old tradition for the village." Sophie said, a sense of satisfaction in her voice.

Lily smiled, her thoughts drifting to the future. "I can't wait to do it again next year. We'll have more time to make it even more magical."

Their stroll through the park turned into a planning session for the next year's event. Ideas flowed freely. They even discussed the idea of a small Christmas market to bring in people from other villages and towns.

As they left the park, they ran into Mrs James, walking her dog. Her face lit up when she saw them. "Lily, Sophie, I've been wanting to thank you. Last night was truly magical. You've brought so much joy to our village. And because of you, the village will have new life breathed into it. The next village meeting I want you two there. We owe you so much. This village will live up to its past, and we will revive a lot more of the old traditions."

The girls beamed with happiness. "Thank you, Mrs James. It wouldn't have been possible without your help, too," Lily replied.

"And the magic of your lantern," Sophie added with a wink.

Mrs James laughed, a twinkle in her eye. "Ah, that old lantern has more stories to tell than you can imagine. I'm glad it could be part of your wonderful night."

"What are we going to do with all these lanterns?" asked Lily.

"That's not a problem. I have organised a clean-up party for this afternoon. They will be cleaned, dried and put away until next year."

Lily and Sophie looked at each other, their faces beaming with joy. As they parted ways, Lily and Sophie continued their walk through the village, their minds buzzing with ideas and their hearts full of the joy they brought to their community. The Winter Garden of Lights had been a success, and they were already dreaming of what the next year would bring.

"We could get one more story in before we have to prepare for tonight," said Lily.

Lily and Sophie, with hearts brimming with newfound belief and wonder, made their way speedily back home. They were ready to venture once more to the Athenaeum, the mystical library room which had been the centre of their extraordinary adventures. As Lily inserted the key into the spine of the book, they were again enveloped in the magical light which transported them into the room. They looked around as an unsettling emptiness greeted them. The room was now bare. The absence of the familiar table, chairs, and the cherished book sent a shiver down their spines.

The girls exchanged puzzled glances, their eyes scanning the room, searching for something, anything, which resembled the Athenaeum they knew. The single hanging lightbulb overhead began to flicker erratically, casting long, dancing shadows against the bare walls. The flickering grew more intense, casting an otherworldly glow that seemed to pulse with a life of its own.

In the midst of this flickering light, Jingles materialised. His appearance, as always, was a blend of mischief and wisdom. His eyes twinkled with a knowing light, and a large smile greeted them.

"Lily and Sophie," Jingles began, his voice echoing slightly in the empty room. "The time has come for you to complete your journey. The Athenaeum and its treasured book have served their purpose. Sophie, your belief in the magic of Christmas has been rekindled, as have your mothers and almost the entire village."

Jingles sighed. "I'm sorry girls, but you must return the magic book to its rightful place in the library and give me back the key. It is essential these items are restored to maintain the balance of magic in the world."

Lily and Sophie looked at each other. Their eyes widened as Jingles' words hit home. They would never be able to come here again. They both experienced a sinking feeling; and together they gasped a sigh of both understanding and disappointment. Lily nodded solemnly.

Jingles looked at the girls and smiled, "Your journey does not end here. This afternoon, you must spread the spirit of Christmas through good deeds around the village. The magic of Christmas is not just in belief but in actions, in spreading joy and kindness to others."

With a snap of his fingers, Jingles enveloped them in a swirl of magical light. The girls felt a gentle warmth wrap around them, a sensation like being wrapped in a soft, glowing blanket. In an instant, they found themselves back in the comforting surroundings of Lily's bedroom. The walls, decked with posters and pictures, the bed's floral quilt, and the desk, a jumble of schoolbooks and trinkets, momentarily paled in comparison to the wonder of the Athenaeum.

Their hearts were heavy with the realisation that their journey through the magical stories had come to an end. 'The History of Our Village', once a portal to countless adventures and enchantments, now lay quiet in their hands, its magic silenced.

With a visible sense of loss, Lily and Sophie slowly made their way back to the library, each step they took feeling heavy, as though laden with the weight of a significant chapter closing in their young lives. The cherished book, nestled in Lily's hands, now held silent pages filled with their shared adventures and memories.

The library, with its vaulted ceilings and endless rows of books, enveloped them in a hushed, reverent atmosphere. It was as if the very walls and shelves within this sanctuary of knowledge had recognised the gravity of their farewell to the book which had become a dear friend.

As they walked through the aisles, their eyes glanced over the spines of countless books, each holding its own world of stories and secrets. The muffled sounds of pages turning and the occasional soft footsteps of other patrons added to the solemn ambience. Sunlight filtered through the tall windows, casting long, soft beams across the polished wooden floor and the rows of bookshelves. Finally, they reached the librarian's desk. Here, the air was still, almost sacred. They stood for a moment, holding the book between them, a silent exchange of reluctant acceptance passing through their eyes. It was more than just returning a book; it was about letting go of a piece of their shared experience, a magical journey that bonded them even closer.

Gently, with a care that spoke volumes of their attachment, they handed the book over to the librarian. She took the book with a gentle, almost reverential touch and smiled softly at them. She placed the book on top of a pile of other returned books, each awaiting its return to the shelves to become part of another person's story. As they walked away from the desk, their steps became lighter. The weight of the moment lifted, and in its place, the hopeful promise of the next chapter in their journey of discovery.

Determined to fulfil Jingles' instructions, Lily and Sophie set out into the village. The winter air was crisp, and the village was a picture of festive cheer with colourful wreaths embellishing doors and windows.

Their first deed was at Mrs Brumble's house, an elderly woman who lived alone. They cleared her path of snow and straightened an old wreath which hung on her door.

Next, they visited the village church, where they helped the vicar tidy the church and lay out hymn books for the evening service.

As the afternoon dimmed into twilight, Lily and Sophie found themselves assisting Mr. Jenkins, the local baker, with his late daily rounds, delivering loaves of freshly baked bread to the villagers. The scent of cinnamon and warm dough drifted over them, a comforting embrace amidst the chill winter air tinged with hints of pine and peppermint. They ambled past the towering Christmas tree in the square, its now decorated boughs glistening in the frosty air.

"Jingles!" Said Sophie, as he just appeared in front of them. "You made me jump. What are you doing here?"

Jingles smiled, "Watch." He pointed skywards.

Sophie and Lily both gasped, their gaze transfixed upwards in rapture. Above them, a singular, radiant star began its slow descent from the heavens, casting a celestial glow which captivated the entire square. The Christmas tree, newly adorned in festive decor, now awaited its crowning glory. As the star settled gently on top of the tree, it began to emit a gentle, pulsating light, unlike any earthly glow. The star's luminescence bathed the tree, casting an aura of pure, soft light which seemed to pulse with the heartbeat of Christmas itself.

Villagers, drawn as if by an unseen force, congregated around the spectacle. Their faces, awash with the star's gentle light, reflected a myriad of emotions, wonder, joy, and an unspoken understanding of something profoundly magical unfolding before their eyes. Children's laughter chimed through the air, their small fingers pointing upwards as the light from the star touched each face.

Lily, standing close to Sophie, noted a surge of warmth emanating from deep within. The star's descent was not just a spectacle of light; it represented the culmination of their efforts, a beacon of the goodwill and unity they had fostered throughout the village. The glow from the star seemed to resonate within her, a reminder of the enduring spirit of community and the shared joy the festive season brings.

The square hummed with soft exclamations and gasps of delight. "How did this happen?" someone murmured, their voice almost lost in the sacred atmosphere. "It's the magic of the season," another replied, their tone imbued with reverence and wonder.

Unseen, yet ever-present, Jingles watched from the shadows, his eyes reflecting the star's gentle glow. "Remember," he whispered, his voice a tender murmur carried on the wintry breeze to Lily and Sophie, "The magic of Christmas is within you, always. Cherish it, spread its light, and it shall illuminate the darkest of winters." With that, he once again vanished in a cloud of sparkling smoke.

As the star continued its gentle pulsation, a hush fell over the square, the usual bustle of village life giving way to a reverent stillness. The light from the star spilled over the edges of the tree, touching every corner of the square with a tender glow. The faces of the villagers upturned and bathed in light. Each wrinkle, each smile, and each wide-eyed stare that previously told a story of disbelief, now told a story of joy. Above them, the sky, a deep velvet expanse stretched out, dotted with stars that seemed to celebrate along with the village below. They twinkled in a quiet chorus, echoing the light of their earthly counterpart.

Sophie, her hand finding Lily's in the crowd, squeezed gently. They shared a smile, their bond deepened by the magic they witnessed and the knowledge they had played a part in this night's enchantment. Around them, the village, usually a simple collection of homes and lives, was transformed into a scene of history, alive with magic and light. Every villager sensed a profound and unspoken promise in that moment. They believed this light, and this magic, would endure even after they passed away. It would serve as a symbol of hope and unity during all future winters.

Lily and Sophie, with infectious smiles, headed for home, their hearts still aglow with the magic they witnessed and nurtured, the crisp night air was filled with the echo of their laughter. The Christmas tree's twinkling lights, symbols of their shared goodwill, receded into the distance, its star still shining skyward.

Upon reaching Lily's home, the girls stepped from one magical moment into the anticipation of another. The warmth of the house welcomed them, a noticeable contrast to the chilly winter air outside. They shed their winter coats and made their way up to Lily's room, their excitement bubbling inside them. The air was charged with the feeling of approaching magic, and their eyes sparkled with the joy of the adventure which awaited them.

The invitation they had received was laid out before them on Lily's bed, its words a promise of a wondrous journey that Lily

107

read aloud once more, "You're invited to the North Pole to meet Santa Claus and discover the magic of Christmas. Be in your room on the night of the 23rd, and all your questions will be answered. P.S. you can bring a friend."

Sophie, her eyes wide with wonder, read the invitation again for what seemed like the hundredth time. "Can you believe this, Lily? We're actually going to meet Santa!"

Lily, her smile as bright as the stars, nodded enthusiastically. "It's like a dream come true. I've always wanted to see the North Pole."

The girls' mothers had given their consent for the sleepover, their amusement and curiosity evident in their smiles. They knew their daughters were embarking on an adventure, one which would be cherished for years to come. For what they had done for the village, and shown Christmas magic really does exist, this was a fitting reward.

As evening approached, Lily and Sophie prepared themselves for their journey. They dressed in their warmest clothes.

"I wonder what the North Pole will be like," Sophie mused, her eyes reflecting the soft glow of Lily's bedside lamp.

"I think it'll be like stepping into a Christmas film," Lily replied, her imagination painting pictures of snow-covered landscapes and twinkling lights.

The girls sat in Lily's room, watching the clock's hands slowly turn about its face, taking what seemed like forever. The room was festooned with festive decorations, a cosy haven filled with the soft glow of fairy lights and the warmth of shared excitement.

As the hours ticked by, seven o'clock, eight o'clock, nine o'clock. The initial surge of enthusiasm waned, replaced by a tinge of tiredness and doubt. Sophie, nestled among the pillows, turned to Lily with a question, her voice tinged with impatience. "When do you think we'll go, Lily? And how do you think it'll happen?"

Lily, lying beside her, her eyes fixed on the clock, sighed softly. "I wish I knew. Maybe it's like in the stories, where magic happens when you least expect it."

The room was quiet, save for the soft ticking of the clock and the gentle breathing of the girls. As the hands of the clock edged closer to midnight, their eyelids grew heavy, and soon, both were lost in a world of dreams, snuggled under the cosy duvet.

The clock struck midnight, and the room was suddenly filled with a soft light which seemed to dance across the walls and ceiling. It was as if the room had been transformed into a realm of enchantment.

"Are you ready for an adventure?" asked a voice, jolly and warm. It was Jingles, the magic Christmas elf, his figure shimmering in the ghostly light.

Sophie stirred first, her eyes fluttering open to the sight of Jingles. She nudged Lily awake, whispering excitedly, "Lily, wake up! It's time!"

Lily blinked open her eyes, and a gasp of delight escaped her lips as she saw Jingles standing there, his eyes twinkling with mirth. "Jingles! You're here!"

Jingles chuckled, his laughter once again like the sound of tinkling bells. "Of course, I'm here! Did you think I'd miss out on such a grand adventure?"

The girls quickly scrambled out of bed, their earlier fatigue forgotten, replaced by a surge of excitement. "We're ready, Jingles. We've been ready all night!" Lily exclaimed, her voice bubbling with enthusiasm.

Jingles nodded, a mischievous smile playing on his lips. "Then hold on tight, for we're about to embark on a journey to the North Pole, to meet Santa Claus himself!"

With a wave of his hand, a swirl of magical light appeared around the girls. They felt the sensation of floating, of being lifted from the ground. Lily's room seemed to blur, its colours and shapes merging into a whirl of light and shadow.

"Here we go!" Jingles announced, and with those words, they were whisked away on their magical journey. The sensation was exhilarating, like riding a gust of wind through a tunnel of shimmering stars and swirling bright colours.

As they travelled through the magical vortex, Lily and Sophie held hands, their eyes wide with wonder. They passed

109

through clouds which shimmered like candyfloss and past stars that sparkled like diamonds in the night sky.

The adventure had begun. With Jingles as their guide, they knew they were in for an unforgettable experience. The promise of meeting Santa Claus, of discovering the magic of Christmas at the North Pole filled their hearts with joy and anticipation.

Their journey through the magical vortex continued, each twist and turn bringing them closer to their destination. The excitement was evident, the magic real, and for Lily and Sophie, this was a night that would be etched in their memories forever.

Chapter 10

As Lily and Sophie blinked through the dazzling light of the magical vortex, they stood in the heart of an enchanting realm beyond their wildest dreams. It was Santa's very own living room. The room glowed with a warm, inviting atmosphere. Delicate fairy lights twinkled from garlands of holly and ivy, punctuating the walls trimmed with rich, red velvet curtains. The air was alive with the aroma of pine from the towering Christmas tree standing majestically in one corner. The tree decorated with lots of different ornaments that looked like crystals, wooden reindeer, and little sleighs. The tree had golden ribbons cascading down its sides, and on top, a magnificent star shimmering with a soft, golden light.

Under the tree, there were many presents wrapped in beautiful paper. Each adorned with silken bows and a tag with a name written in Santa's own handwriting. The logs in the fireplace crackled, filling the room with a comforting sound. The flames danced merrily, casting a warm, amber glow over the plush, red and green carpet.

Overhead, the ceiling was painted like the night sky, dotted with tiny, twinkling stars that appeared to gently pulse with their own magical light. The windows were frosted at the edges. They framed the winter wonderland outside, where the Northern Lights danced across the sky in a spectacular display of green, red, and purple.

The air was infused with the sweet scent of gingerbread and cinnamon, emanating from a large batch of cookies cooling on a table near the hearth. Next to them was a steaming pot of hot chocolate. Two mugs had already been poured with a mountain of whipped cream topped with marshmallows and chocolate chips floating on top. It looked so good they could taste it.

A large, ornate chair stood next to the fireplace. It was upholstered in red velvet and trimmed with white fur. The chair had a high back, which was crowned with a glistening garland of evergreens and red berries. This was Santa's chair, instilled with an air of majesty and timeless tradition.

111

Lily and Sophie stood there, their eyes wide with astonishment, drinking in every detail of this magical room. The sights, the sounds, the smells, all conspired to create a moment so perfect, so full of Christmas spirit, it felt like they had stepped into a living dream.

Lily and Sophie's eyes widened as they heard a familiar distant sound. "Ho! Ho! Ho!"

They turned to each other in excitement and clasped each other's hand, their hearts beating wildly as they heard the approaching footsteps.

The Christmas magic around them was momentarily interrupted by the deep, joyous sound echoing through the room once again, "Ho! Ho! Ho! Lily and Sophie looked at each other, their hearts racing, eyes gleaming with unspoken joy.

With tightly clasped hands, they shared an exhilarating moment as footsteps approached. Each step filling the room with anticipation. The crackling fire danced joyfully, and the twinkling lights glowed even brighter, as if eagerly anticipating Santa's arrival.

The aroma of gingerbread and cinnamon mingled with the warmth of the room appeared to become more noticeable. The footsteps ceased, the air seemed to hold its breath. Then, into the room, stepped Santa Claus himself. He was a grand presence, matching the legends. Dressed in red, with a white, fluffy beard, and twinkling eyes behind gold-rimmed glasses.

Lily's and Sophie's faces lit up with pure joy as they beheld the iconic figure. Santa's jovial smile and the warmth in his eyes welcomed them, a silent assurance they were exactly where they were meant to be. This was not just a meeting with a legendary figure; it was a culmination of their journey of belief, a moment where magic and reality danced together in perfect harmony.

Santa approached, his laughter still echoing in the room. The girls felt the magic of Christmas envelop them. It was a feeling so profound and beautiful that it transcended words. They stood there, hand in hand, in the heart of Christmas itself, their spirits soaring with the joy and wonder of the season.

"Hello Santa." Said Jingles, breaking the silence.

Santa gave a courteous nod. "Hello Jingles, and hello Lily and Sophie." His voice was deep and welcoming.

Lily opened her mouth to speak, but the words tangled in her throat like a knot she couldn't loosen. Her heart raced, pounding so loud she thought for a moment Santa might hear it. Her fingers trembled as they curled around the warm mug of hot chocolate, yet her tongue felt too heavy, too dry, to form the words she so desperately wanted to say.

"Relax... relax, my dear," Santa's voice was as soft as freshly fallen snow. "Please, sit and enjoy your hot chocolate. I had it specially prepared for your arrival. I do hope it's as good as Mrs James' famous recipe."

At the mention of Mrs James, Lily's eyes flickered with surprise. Her fingers tightened on the handle of her mug. She exchanged a quick, wide-eyed glance with Sophie. Mrs James' hot chocolate was a secret, how could he possibly know about it?

"How... would he know that?" Lily whispered, her breath barely stirring the air between them.

Sophie shifted uncomfortably, her own voice coming out in a halting whisper, "I'm... I'm sure it's just as good as Mrs James' hot chocolate." She forced a nervous smile, her cheeks flushing as she stammered.

Santa chuckled softly, the sound deep and reassuring, like a cosy fire crackling in a hearth. He leaned back in his plush chair, the gentle twinkle in his eyes never wavering. Jingles, Santa's ever-mischievous elf, snapped his fingers with a grin. In an instant, two chairs appeared beside Santa's, their cushions plump and inviting, waiting for the girls to sit.

"Come now, don't be shy," Santa urged with that same kind smile, his rosy cheeks glowing. "Sit, drink your chocolate while it's still warm. There's plenty more in the pot if you'd like seconds."

The girls hesitated, still in awe, but the aroma of the rich, creamy hot chocolate was too tempting to resist. Slowly, they sat down, the chairs soft beneath them, almost as if they were sitting on clouds. Lily took a cautious sip of the chocolate. The sweetness, the warmth, it was like being wrapped in the most comforting memory. Her nerves began to ease, the tightness in her throat loosening with every sip.

Sophie glanced at Santa, her curiosity sparking as the warmth from the drink spread through her. "How did you know about Mrs James and her hot chocolate?" she finally asked, her voice stronger now, though still laced with wonder.

Santa smiled knowingly, his eyes twinkling with a secret only he seemed to know. "Ah, my dear, there are many things I know. I watch over all the children, and I learn the little things that bring them joy. And for you two, I knew nothing could calm your nerves like a cup of Mrs James' famous hot chocolate, but with my own little twist... peppermint."

Lily and Sophie exchanged another glance, the mystery swirling between them like the steam rising from their mugs. But somehow, the strangeness of it all didn't feel unsettling anymore. In fact, it felt... magical.

Hand in hand, Lily, and Sophie tentatively made their way towards the chairs that appeared next to Santa's majestic throne. Their hearts pounded with a mixture of excitement and admiration as they took their seats, the plush cushions feeling like soft clouds beneath them. The room, with its festive atmosphere, seemed to embrace them even more. While the warmth from the fireplace gently caressed their cheeks.

Jingles, with a twinkle in his eye, gestured towards the steaming mugs of hot chocolate. "Go on, girls. It's not every day you get to enjoy Santa's special hot chocolate. Have some more."

Lily, her nervousness easing slightly, reached for a second mug. The rich aroma of chocolate mixed with a hint of peppermint filled her senses, bringing a smile to her face. Sophie followed suit, her eyes lighting up as she took another tentative sip. The hot chocolate was creamy and smooth, with just the right amount of peppermint, a perfect concoction. Jingles smiled, clicked his fingers and vanished in a cloud of sparkles.

"This is amazing, Santa!" Sophie exclaimed, her earlier stutter forgotten in her delight. "We'll have to tell Mrs James about the peppermint." She continued.

Santa chuckled, his eyes crinkling with mirth. "I'm glad you like it, Sophie. Now, tell me, what brings two such brave and adventurous girls to the North Pole on this fine evening?"

Lily, finding her voice, spoke up. "We received your invitation, Santa. It said to be here on the night of the 23rd to discover the magic of Christmas."

Santa nodded, his gaze warm and knowing. "Ah, yes, the invitation. Every year, I select a few special children who have shown exceptional kindness and belief in the magic of Christmas. These chosen ones get to spend some time with me at the North Pole. You two have spread so much joy and goodwill in your village. It's only fitting you experience the heart of Christmas here at the North Pole."

Sophie's eyes sparkled with curiosity. "But why us, Santa? There are so many other deserving children."

Santa leaned forward, his voice soft but filled with sincerity. "Every child is special, Sophie. But you and Lily have a rare gift. You not only believe in the magic of Christmas, but you also embody its true spirit through your actions. You've touched the hearts of many with your good deeds. And, you are from Santclausby. That was one of my first magical villages, but sadly people lost the faith and it lost its magic. That is, until you two revived it."

Lily and Sophie exchanged glances, a sense of pride and happiness blooming within them. Their adventures and efforts to spread joy were being recognised in the most magical way possible.

Jingles appeared in the middle of the room. "Santa!" He interrupted, his voice tinged with concern. "I'm terribly sorry to disturb you, but this has just arrived. It was marked URGENT by the elves," he said, handing a scroll to Santa. With a solemn nod, Santa unfurled the parchment, revealing a handwritten letter from a boy named Charlie:

"Is everything alright, Santa?" Jingles asked, noting the worry on Santa's face as he read the letter.

Santa's voice was heavy with emotion as he read Charlie's words aloud, silencing the room.

"Dear Santa,

115

I don't know if you remember me, but I'm now staying with the Johannson's. They're really kind. Since my new dad lost his job, we've barely had enough warmth, and food is scarce. I overheard them say we can't have Christmas this year as the money is nearly all gone. Mrs Johannson tries to hide her tears, but we see her sadness. I don't need gifts for myself, I would gladly go without, but could you bring some joy to my new family? They've done so much for me, even though they have so little for themselves.

Thank you,

Charlie."

Santa looked up from the scroll. "We can't wait until Christmas Eve, Jingles. They need our help immediately," Santa declared with resolve. "Tonight, we'll deliver a parcel full of food, gifts for the children, and a few extra things to help them through these difficult times."

"Tonight, sir? But it's only the 23rd!" exclaimed Jingles.

"Yes, tonight," Santa affirmed. "The Johannson's have sacrificed so much for Charlie. It's our turn to ensure their Christmas is filled with hope, not despair."

Santa sighed deeply, his heart aching. "The Johannson family, Jingles. Despite their dwindling finances, they've shared everything with Charlie, keeping him safe, fed and warm."

Jingles's expression mirrored Santa's distress. "That's incredibly generous of them."

"Yes, it is. Their father has just lost his job, and with hardly any money left and Christmas so near, they can barely afford to keep a fire burning in the hearth."

Jingles gasped, "That's dreadful."

"Santa," stared Lily, "How can today be the 23rd? We came here at midnight on the 23rd, that should make this morning Christmas eve."

Santa smiled, that's the magic of the North Pole, time runs differently here."

The girls looked at each other, confusion written on their faces.

Santa smiled and turned to Lily and Sophie. "Tonight, you will not only witness the magic of Christmas, but also play a crucial part in it. I have a special task that needs your unique talents."

The girls leaned in, their faces alight with curiosity and eagerness. "What kind of task, Santa?" Lily asked, her voice brimming with enthusiasm.

Santa's eyes sparkled knowingly. "As you're aware, Christmas is about more than just receiving; it's about giving, sharing, and bringing joy. This year, there's a family in dire need of our help. They're not far away, in a small village, and they could really use a burst of happiness. I'm asking you two to help me deliver a special gift that could make all the difference."

Sophie's eyes shone with excitement. "We'd be honoured to help, Santa! But how will we manage it? And won't people see you?"

"No, we won't be seen. My sleigh is magic, it cannot be seen during the day." Santa smiled, pleased with their readiness to help. "With a sprinkle of magic and your boundless spirit, I'm certain we'll make it a Christmas to remember for them. You'll ride with me tonight, and together, we'll ensure this family feels the love and warmth of the season."

Santa's smile widened. "With a little of North Pole magic and the help of my reindeer, of course. But first, you must prepare. Jingles, would you show them to the wardrobe room?"

Jingles nodded and stood up, his bell jingling merrily. "Of course, right this way girls."

The girls followed Jingles out of the living room and down a long, twinkling corridor decorated with portraits of past Christmases at the North Pole. They arrived at a large door ornately carved with images of snowflakes and reindeer.

As the door swung open, they stepped into a room filled with racks upon racks of winter clothing in every imaginable colour and style. There were cosy sweaters, fluffy scarves, and an array of hats and mittens. Jingles guided them to two outfits, perfectly sized.

"These will keep you warm and comfortable on your journey," Jingles explained, helping them into the thick, fur-lined coats and snug boots.

117

Once they were dressed, they looked like true North Pole adventurers, ready for whatever magical task lay ahead. The girls looked different in the mirror, not just in their clothes, but also in their excitement for the adventure that lay ahead.

Jingles clasped his hands together. "Perfect! Now, let's get you to Santa's sleigh. Your Christmas mission awaits!"

The girls were wrapped up warmly and filled with excitement. They followed Jingles back to Santa's living room. Their hearts were beating fast in anticipation of what was to come. This visit to the North Pole was more than just a trip. It was an opportunity to experience the magic they now believed in. It was a chance to make a meaningful impact and bring joy to others, embracing the genuine spirit of Christmas.

The journey back to Santa's living room was a blur of both excitement and anticipation for Lily and Sophie. Their steps quickened as they imagined the adventure that awaited them. When they entered the living room, Santa was waiting, his face beaming with a warm, welcoming smile.

"Ah, you look ready for a true North Pole adventure!" Santa exclaimed, his eyes sparkling with delight.

The girls giggled, their eyes shining with excitement. "We are ready, Santa!" Lily declared, her voice strong and confident.

Santa led them outside, where the sky was illuminated by the mesmerising dance of the Northern Lights. The air was crisp, filled with the scent of pine and the distant sound of Christmas carols. Santa's magnificent sleigh stood before them. It was resplendent in red and gold. Its polished silver runners gleaming.

The reindeer, harnessed and ready to go, pawed at the ground eagerly, their breaths forming little clouds in the cold air. Their antlers and leather reins were adorned with small silver bells which gently rang out in the crisp night air, adding to the festive atmosphere.

"Climb aboard," Santa said, gesturing towards the sleigh. "Tonight, you are part of a very special Christmas mission."

The girls climbed into the sleigh, their hearts pounding with excitement. Santa took his place at the front, holding the reins with practiced ease. With a hearty "Ho! Ho! Ho!" and a flick of the reins, the sleigh gently moved forward before being lifted off the ground, gliding effortlessly into the shimmering sky.

The sensation was exhilarating. Their faces were brushed by the icy wind. The world below transformed into a patchwork of lights and shadows. The girls held on tightly. Their eyes were wide with wonder. They soared over snow-covered mountains. Flying over dense forests, they continued their journey. They passed sleepy villages. Everything was blanketed in the serene calm of a winter's day.

As they soared through the skies, Santa shared a heartfelt story. "In their humble dwelling, the glow of candlelight dances across worn wooden furniture and threadbare rugs," he started. His voice carried warmth and admiration. "This family, though possessing little, has generously given much. The aroma of a simple homemade soup permeates the kitchen, a symbol of their now meagre existence and of their open-heartedness. Despite limited resources, they consistently made space for an extra person at their table, going so far as to wrap a young boy in their blankets for warmth. Now, with Christmas approaching, their immense kindness has left them with little to celebrate the season. Yet, they've asked for nothing, offering everything with open hearts. They truly embody the spirit of Christmas. They deserve a celebration that mirrors the immense joy they've given to that young boy Charlie. This family has extended their love so freely, especially to the boy who has found safety in their care. They deserve to experience the magic of Christmas that they have generously given to others." He paused, allowing the weight of their generosity to sink in.

"But... How do you know what's happening inside their home?" asked Sophie.

Santa turned to look at Sophie. He merely smiled and replied, "Because I'm Santa."

With a flick of the reins, Santa encouraged the reindeer to fly faster while the girls held on tightly. After a few minutes, the sleigh descended towards a small, quaint village nestled in a valley. The houses were adorned with lights and decorations, but one house, in particular, stood out. It was modest and dimly lit, with no sign of festive cheer.

"This is the house," Santa whispered, guiding the sleigh to land softly nearby. "This is but a small tribute to the immense generosity they've shown," he said, handing them a sack of beautifully wrapped packages. "It's not just a gift; it's a symbol of hope, love, and the spirit of Christmas."

Santa instructed Lily and Sophie to hold the sack of gifts while he waited out of sight. He emphasised the need to keep his presence and the origin of the gifts a secret.

"Yes Santa, you can trust us," Lilly replied.

With the crunch of snow under their boots, they approached the front door. Sophie gave a firm knock, and waited, their hearts filled with a mix of nervousness and excitement.

A woman opened the door, her face etched with the traces of hardship, which softened into an expression of gentle surprise as she looked upon Lily and Sophie. The sight of the girls, laden with a sack brimming with food and presents, brought a flicker of disbelief and hope to her weary eyes. Behind her, two curious children peeked out, their gazes wide with wonder.

"Merry Christmas!" Lily and Sophie said as one, their voices carrying the warmth and cheer of the season.

"We've brought something special for you," Sophie said softly, extending the sack towards the woman. "These are gifts to brighten your Christmas."

The woman, visibly touched, reached out with trembling hands to accept the sack. Tears welled up in her eyes, each a shimmering testimony to her gratitude. "Oh, thank you," she whispered, her voice laden with emotion, "But who are they from?"

"From someone who wants to reward your generosity," Said Lily with a warming smile.

The lady gestured them inside, where Lily and Sophie entered the candlelit kitchen. It was just as Santa described, soft shadows were playing across simple wooden furniture, and threadbare rugs, lending a warm glow to the room. Cooking utensils dangled from the walls, and earthenware pots sat on a crackling wood-fired stove, filling the air with the savoury scent of fish soup. Earthy aromas of potatoes, carrots, and turnips hinted at their humble meal. A hand-sewn curtain fluttered slightly at a broken window, the room a testament to thier resilience and simplicity of living. Charlie and his older sister watched in anticipation as Lily and Sophie began to empty the sack, they revealed parcels wrapped in festive paper. There was food, fresh bread, fruits, and presents for the whole family. The excitement in the air was evident as the family watched, wide-eyed and overwhelmed by the unexpected bounty.

The final gift, a large brown envelope wrapped with a tag urging 'Open it today', was handed to Mrs Johannson. Her hands trembled with anticipation as she unwrapped it, revealing a bundle of money. Tears streamed down her cheeks as she stammered, "I cannot accept this. This is far too generous. Who could be so kind?"

"It's for you. Please accept it, we cannot take it back. And we promised not to tell you who it is from."

Mrs Johannson clasped the envelope with both hands holding it close to her heart as tears streamed down her face. The joy and gratitude radiating from her family was unmistakable. They huddled closer, their faces alight with wonder and astonishment. Lily and Sophie watched, their hearts swelling with happiness at the joy they had brought to this humble home, their spirits lifted by the pure, heartfelt gratitude of the family.

"Would you like to stay and share some soup with us?"

"That is very kind of you," said Lily with a smile, "but we must get back home."

The modest room, initially dim and unadorned, suddenly seemed full of light and the warmth of the season. Laughter and excited chatter echoed off the walls, creating a room of happiness and shared humanity. The girls revelled in the family's joy, their hearts swelling with the satisfaction of bringing happiness to others.

It was time to leave. The girls waved their goodbyes. The sight of the gratitude and tears in the woman's eyes were a gift Lily and Sophie would carry in their hearts forever. Beside her, the father placed a comforting hand on her shoulder, his own emotions reflected in his eyes. He looked at his children, their faces alight with wonder and disbelief, he felt a profound gratitude swell within him. This gift was more than just a relief from their struggles; it was a reminder of the goodness in the world, of hope in times of despair. Charlie, the young boy, the newest member of their family, watched in awe. Until now, his life had been a patchwork of uncertainties. But in this moment, surrounded by love and witnessing such unexpected kindness, he felt a sense of belonging he'd never dared to dream of before. "I think I know where these things came from," he thought to himself, looking up at the shimmering sky, "Thank you Santa." he whispered.

The family came together, their embraces a silent witness to the impact of the girls' actions. In this simple but profound act of giving, Sophie and Lily had not just brightened their Christmas but had woven a stronger bond within the whole family. A reminder that even in the bleakest of times, there is light, there is love, and above all, there is hope.

The girls walked away, the empty sack in their hands. "We are so lucky to have what we have at home," said Sophie. A tear lodged itself in Lily's eye. "It makes you feel so grateful, doesn't it?" Lily's voice trembled as she spoke, each word soaked with a mixture of appreciation and sorrow. Sophie nodded, her own eyes glinting with a similar sheen of unshed tears. Sophie squeezed Lily's hand. "Yes, very grateful," she affirmed, her voice a soft whisper carried away by the gentle breeze, leaving a solemn pact of gratitude hanging between them.

Lily and Sophie, still buzzing from the excitement of their task, nestled into the cosy, plush seats of Santa's sleigh. As the sleigh began to rise, the air grew colder, nipping at their cheeks, but it was a refreshing kind of chill, one that made them feel alive, invigorated by the magic surrounding them. Santa took the reins with a gentle tug, guiding the reindeer higher into the sky. "Hold on tight, girls," he said, his eyes twinkling with mischief. "We're going to take the scenic route home."

The sleigh soared upward, and suddenly they were gliding above a vast expanse of glistening white. The snow-covered landscape of the North Pole stretched out beneath them, untouched and pure, sparkling like a field of diamonds. The silence up here was profound, only broken by the soft jingle of the reindeer's bells, each chime echoing across the frozen wilderness below.

"Look over there!" Santa pointed, his thick glove extending toward the horizon. Lily and Sophie craned their necks, and their eyes widened in amazement. In the distance, an icy castle rose from the snow, its towering spires made of translucent ice that shimmered with every colour of the rainbow. It stood proudly against the sky, the soft glow of the Northern Lights reflecting off its crystalline walls, making it seem almost otherworldly.

"That's the Ice Palace," Santa explained. "It's where the Ice Fairies live. They're the ones who paint the frost on your windows every winter morning."

As they flew closer, the girls could see tiny, fluttering figures darting around the palace, their wings glistening in the light. The fairies waved as the sleigh passed by, their laughter echoing like the softest chimes on the wind. Sophie gasped, her eyes sparkling as brightly as the ice below. "They're so beautiful!"

Lily nodded, captivated by the sight, but before they could say another word, the sleigh dipped lower, and they were skimming across the surface of the frozen sea. In the distance, enormous sheets of ice shifted and cracked, the sound resonating through the stillness like distant thunder. Then, just as they passed over a particularly large iceberg, they saw them... polar bears. A mother bear and her two cubs ambled across the ice, their thick, white fur blending in with the snow. The cubs tumbled and played, chasing each other with clumsy, endearing steps, while the mother watched with a patient, protective gaze. Sophie clapped her hands together, barely containing her excitement. "Look, Lily! Real polar bears!"

Santa chuckled, steering the sleigh around them. "The North Pole is full of surprises. It's not just about toys and presents. There's a whole world of magic out here."

As they continued their journey, the sky began to darken, and the stars emerged one by one, blinking into existence like tiny, silver lanterns scattered across a velvet blanket. The moon hung low in the sky, full and radiant, casting a soft, silvery light over the landscape below. Every breath the girls exhaled seemed to crystallise in the air, twinkling briefly before vanishing into the night. Soon, they passed over the Enchanted

Forest, a hidden grove where the fir trees sparkled as if each branch had been dipped in stardust. The pine needles glistened with frost, and faint, luminous creatures darted between the trees, tiny woodland sprites that left trails of glittering light in their wake. Lily and Sophie watched in awe as one sprite flew up to the sleigh, pausing just long enough to wave before diving back into the forest below. The Northern Lights above seemed to dance in celebration of their achievement, ribbons of green, violet, and soft blue unfurling across the sky in shimmering waves.

"I didn't know there were trees at the North Pole, Santa," Lily exclaimed, her eyes wide with wonder.

"There is only one magical forest," Santa replied, his voice taking on a deeper, more mysterious tone. "The Enchanted Forest is unique, and it is older than even I am. It hides within the snow, waiting for the right moment to show itself. You see, it doesn't appear for just anyone."

The girls exchanged glances, feeling a thrill at the thought that they had been chosen to see something so rare and wondrous. "Why did it show itself to us?" Sophie asked.

Santa smiled warmly. "The forest reveals itself to those who carry kindness in their hearts, those who believe in the magic of the world around them."

"Almost home," Santa murmured, and the girls felt a pang of longing, wishing this journey could go on forever.

Upon their return, Santa's village welcomed them with its enchanting lights and the merry sound of elves hard at work. They landed smoothly and Santa led them back into the warmth of his cosy living room. The fire crackled invitingly as they settled down to mugs of steaming hot chocolate. Holding the mugs in two hands, they warmed themselves, while smelling the rich chocolaty aroma mingling with the scent of pine and gingerbread.

As they sipped their hot chocolate, and nibbled at the gingerbread, their eyes were heavy with sleep but hearts light with fulfilment. Jingles appeared, his bell jingling softly. "It's time for bed, young adventurers," he said with a gentle smile. "I've prepared a room for you."

Jingles led them down a hallway decorated with paintings of the reindeer and Santa's sleigh. They arrived at a door, behind which lay a room that seemed straight out of a fairy tale. Two carved wooden beds with elegant, red, and green quilts awaited them. The window offered a view of the Northern Lights, painting the sky in vibrant hues.

"Sleep well, Lily and Sophie," Jingles said, "Dream of all the good you've done, and the joy you've brought to others. Tomorrow is going to be another busy day."

As he closed the door, the room was bathed in the soft, magical glow from the Northern Lights, creating a serene and enchanting atmosphere. The girls climbed into their beds, the events of the day replaying in their minds. They whispered to each other about their adventure, their voices a soft murmur in the quiet room.

"Can you believe we actually helped Santa?" Sophie whispered, her voice filled with amazement.

"And we flew in his sleigh!" giggled Lily, her eyes shining in the dim light. "This has been the best day ever."

Their conversation slowly faded as sleep began to claim them. The warmth of the room, the comfortable beds, and the magic of the night enveloped them in a peaceful slumber. Outside, the stars twinkled in the clear sky, and the Northern Lights danced in a display of spectacular beauty. Sophie snuggled down under her warm blankets and drifted into the dream-world. In Sophie's dream, the Northern Lights painted the sky in dazzling colours, casting an ethereal glow over a snow-covered landscape. She stood in a clearing, the crisp air alive with the melody of distant sleigh bells. The surrounding snow shimmered, each flake a tiny mirror reflecting the celestial dance above. Sophie's path led her to a majestic ice castle, its spires glowing with an inner light. As the gates swung open, she was greeted by the sight of a grand hall adorned with sculptures of reindeer and elves, each carved from ice yet seemingly alive. Venturing deeper into the castle, Sophie discovered a room brimming with toys and gifts destined for children around the world. There, in the heart of this enchanted realm, stood Santa. But unlike the jolly figure she knew, Santa appeared weary, his usual sparkle dimmed by illness.

125

"Ah, Sophie," Santa's voice was a mere whisper in the chilled air. "I'm afraid I've fallen ill, and Christmas is in jeopardy."

Panic filled the room as elves were upset, their faces etched with worry. "Christmas might be ruined," they whispered, their usual cheer replaced by despair. But in the dream, Sophie rose to the occasion. "We won't let Christmas be ruined," she declared, her voice steady and full of determination. With Lily by her side, Sophie took charge, rallying the elves with a leader's confidence. "We will deliver the presents," she announced, "and ensure that Christmas is as magical as ever."

Under Sophie's guidance, the elves' panic gave way to calm purpose. They worked tirelessly, packing the sleigh with gifts. And when the night of Christmas Eve arrived, Sophie and Lily, driven by a sense of duty and compassion, took the reins. As they soared through the night sky, the dream showed Sophie the influence of their journey. Houses lit up with joy as presents were delivered, children's laughter echoing in the night's stillness. The dream transformed into a vivid tapestry of happiness and gratitude, a testament to their efforts. Santa, watching from his icy chamber, smiled weakly but with immense pride. "You've done it, Sophie. You and Lily have saved Christmas."

The dream faded. Reality's gentle embrace took hold. Sophie found herself back in the cosy room. The soft glow of the Northern Lights streamed through the window. Lily, still rubbing the sleep from her eyes, turned to her friend, sensing the excitement in Sophie's voice.

"I had the most amazing dream," Sophie began; her eyes alight with the vivid memories of her nocturnal adventure. She recounted every detail, from the sparkling snow under the Northern Lights to the magnificent ice castle and the room filled with gifts. Lily was all ears as Sophie explained Santa was sick and the elves were freaking out, scared that Christmas would be ruined.

"And then," Sophie continued, her voice brimming with pride, "I became the leader of the elves, and we, Lily, we took on Santa's duty to deliver all the presents."

126

Lily was amazed as Sophie painted a picture of their daring flight through the night sky. They were on a sleigh, carrying gifts for children all around the world. Sophie felt the same sense of purpose and determination as Lily. Together, they made sure every present reached its rightful place, keeping the magic of Christmas alive.

"The best part," Sophie said, her voice softening, "was seeing the joy and happiness our actions brought. It was as if the dream was reminding us of the impact kindness and courage can have, especially in times of uncertainty."

Lily, moved by the story, smiled warmly at Sophie. "It sounds like we were actual heroes," she mused, the glow from the Northern Lights reflecting in her eyes.

"Yes," Sophie agreed, her heart full of joy. "And it felt so real."

The girls sat in silence for a moment, lost in thought. As the soft light of dawn filtered through the window, Lily and Sophie sat side by side on their beds, the quiet excitement of a new day blending seamlessly with the tranquillity of the North Pole's twilight.

"Lily, do you think our actions last night will leave a lasting mark?" Sophie queried, her voice reflecting the mixture of hope and doubt which often accompanies meaningful deeds.

Lily turned towards Sophie, her gaze filled with understanding and assurance. "Absolutely. We did more than just hand out presents; we spread hope and joy. That's the essence of Christmas, isn't it?"

Sophie smiled, comforted by Lily's confidence. "You're right. Sometimes, I forget that even the smallest acts can make a big difference."

"And do you recall what Santa mentioned?" Lily gently reminded. "No act of kindness is too small. It all contributes to the greater good."

Sophie mulled over Lily's words, feeling her initial doubts dissipate. "It's like we are part of something much bigger than ourselves."

"That's the point," Lily said, her conviction shining through. "But it's not only about last night. It's about holding onto this spirit of giving and kindness, wherever we go."

Sophie's smile widened, inspired by Lily's insight. "Lily, you have a way of making everything seem possible. I'm so thankful we are sharing this journey together."

Lily reached out, her hand finding Sophie's in a comforting grip. "I am too. Together, we make an awesome team. Who knows what adventures await us today?"

Their laughter filled the room, evidence to the strength and depth of their friendship. It was clear, regardless of what the future held, Lily and Sophie would face it together, their bond was unbreakable.

there was a knock at the door.

Chapter 11

The morning of Christmas Eve dawned bright and cheerful at the North Pole. The air filled with excitement and the faint sound of jingle bells in the distance. Lily and Sophie were gently roused from their dreams of magical reindeer and twinkling lights by a familiar ringing sound. Jingles, ever punctual and merry, knocked at their door.

"Breakfast is ready!" he announced, his voice echoing with joy.

The girls, quickly dressed in fluffy Christmas sweaters and followed Jingles through the winding, festive corridors of Santa's home. The smell of a hearty breakfast wafted through the air, guiding them to the dining room.

As they entered, their eyes widened at the sight before them. The breakfast table was a feast for the senses, laden with all manner of festive goodies. There were stacks of chocolate pancakes, bowls of fresh strawberries, plates of warm, buttery pastries, and a golden, honey-glazed ham. The room was filled with the rich smell of cinnamon, nutmeg, and freshly baked bread, mingling with the ever-present scent of pine.

Santa, already seated at the head of the table, greeted them with a jolly "Good morning!" His eyes twinkled merrily as he motioned for them to join him. "Please sit, have some breakfast. We have a busy day ahead."

The girls, still a little groggy from sleep, eagerly took their seats. Before they could even reach for the maple syrup, Mrs Claus entered, her presence like a warm hug. She carried two steaming mugs of hot peppermint chocolate, the steam rising in delicate swirls.

"Here you go, my dears," Mrs Claus said, placing the mugs before Lily and Sophie. "A special treat to start your day. I'm sorry I was not here to greet you yesterday, I had to go to the hospital with one of the elves."

"I hope it was nothing serious." said Sophie, looking a little concerned.

"Two of the elves were in a candy cane jousting competition and it got a bit too competitive. No serious harm done, cuts and bruises mainly."

"When will they learn." Chuckled Santa.

Sophie took a sip of her hot chocolate and immediately sighed in contentment. "This is amazing, Mrs Claus! Thank you!"

Lily, tasting her own mug of hot chocolate, nodded in agreement. "It's like Christmas in a mug!"

Sitting at the breakfast table, Sophie told Santa about her dream. He listened intently as Sophie recounted it in every detail. Santa paused for a moment, then asked, "Do you think your dream had a meaning?"

Sophie hesitated for a moment. "It was a message. The true spirit of Christmas is not just in giving but in overcoming challenges together, ensuring joy and hope shines bright for all."

Santa sat upright, a proud smile protruded from behind his bushy white beard. "Exactly."

Sophie turned to Lily. "I have you to thank for all this. I lost my belief in Christmas, and it was you who gave it back to me. Without you, I would have missed all the things we have done together."

"Thank you Sophie, but I'm sure you would have done the same for me if the roles were reversed."

Sophie reached across the table, giving Lily's hand a gentle squeeze, their friendship sealed by this shared journey. "Maybe," she smiled, "but it was you who showed me the true meaning of Christmas."

Santa, who had been listening with a twinkle in his eye, nodded approvingly. "You see, it's not the grand gestures that make Christmas special. It's the love, the kindness, and the courage to stand by each other that truly counts."

The girls smiled, taking in Santa's words, feeling a new sense of purpose. They understood now more than ever the power of their actions, no matter how small they might seem. As breakfast came to an end, Santa stood up, his presence commanding the room. "Today," he announced, "we have a lot of preparations for Christmas. I could use your help, would you both like a tour of the workshops?"

"Yes please." They said in unison.

After indulging in a sumptuous morning feast, Santa, his eyes alight with the promise of wonders yet to be revealed, beckoned Lily and Sophie forward. With a hearty chuckle that echoed through the festive halls of the North Pole, he ushered them towards the elves grand dining hall, aglow with the warm radiance of flickering candles and bedecked with boughs of holly and twinkling ornaments. Around the table sat a merry band of elves. Their cheeks rosy with excitement and their bell-adorned hats bobbing and ringing with each exuberant laugh, amused one another with tales of toy-making triumphs and cookie-baking escapades. The air was alive with laughter mingling with the crisp tang of winter's breath that danced in through the open frost-kissed windows.

With each passing moment, the bonds of friendship and camaraderie deepened, as Lily and Sophie found themselves swept up in the infectious spirit of Christmas cheer permeating the room.

And as the morning sun cast its golden rays upon the snowy landscape outside, painting the world in hues of amber and pink, Santa rose from his seat, his eyes ablaze with the fire of anticipation. With a hearty laugh that reverberated through the rafters, he led Lily and Sophie towards the workshops.

As they stepped through the grand doors leading into the workshop, the girls were immediately enveloped by a symphony of sights, sounds, and smells which captured the very essence of Christmas. The workshop was enormous, and it buzzed with a vibrant energy, the pulsating heart of the North Pole where dreams were crafted into reality, this was the main workshop. The air was alive with the rhythmic hum of machinery, the whirring of gears, and the merry clatter of elves using a variety of tools. The elves themselves adorned in their festive green and red attire, scurried between workstations, their nimble fingers a blur as they assembled, painted, and packaged toys with practiced ease.

131

Intermittent wafts of gingerbread, cinnamon, and marzipan coming from the nearby kitchens added a delightful layer to the smell of varnish and paint in the workshop.

A joyful elf, positioned at a large, cluttered desk near the entrance of Santa's bustling workshop, was engaged in a task of immense importance. Her fingers deftly flicked through a towering pile of letters sent by children from around the globe, each one expressing heartfelt wishes and dreams addressed to Santa Claus. The desk was strewn with colourful envelopes of all sizes, decorated with festive stickers, glitter, and the occasionally wobbly handwriting of a child eager to share their Christmas hopes. As she sorted each letter, the elf's eyes scanned the contents with a mixture of concentration and delight. She was responsible for categorising the letters into different types, some asking for toys, others for books, and yet more for special wishes that tugged at heartstrings. Her task didn't just involve sorting, but also flagging-up certain letters that needed Santa's special attention, requests that were unique or particularly touching. After they were prioritised they would be passed onto another letter sorting area for double checking, making sure no child was overlooked.

Next to her, a large Pinboard displayed a map of the world, dotted with pins in various colours representing different types of gifts and the logistics of delivering them. Occasionally, she would pause to pin a letter onto the board, marking it for a special stop along Santa's route. Her workstation was equipped with various tools: magnifying glasses for reading smaller print, stamps for marking processed letters, and a database of all children who had written in previous years. This helped ensure that each child's history with Santa was considered when preparing this year's gifts.

The elf also took the time to write brief notes to Santa about certain letters, highlighting any significant changes from the previous year or any particular need or kindness shown by a child. It was a job that required a keen eye, a warm heart, and an unwavering dedication to the spirit of Christmas, ensuring that every child felt heard and valued by Santa Claus.

Sophie, her eyes wide with amazement, tugged at Lily's sleeve. "Look at that!" she exclaimed, pointing towards a group of elves assembling what appeared to be a miniature train set. The precise detail on each carriage and the glossy finish of the paint were a tribute to the elves' craftsmanship.

Lily's attention, meanwhile, was drawn to a machine which seemed to be knitting Christmas sweaters at an astonishing speed. Each one emerging with intricate patterns and vibrant colours. "It's incredible," she whispered, her voice filled with admiration.

Santa chuckled, his eyes twinkling with pride. "This is where the magic happens," he said, guiding them further into the workshop. "Every toy, every gift, is made with love and care, and a sprinkle of Christmas magic."

They saw a painting station where elves with delicate brushes added finishing touches to dolls and figurines, their hands moving with precision and grace. The concentration on their faces was apparent, each stroke of the brush bringing the toys to life. Sophie, her eyes alight with curiosity and wonder, approached the painting station, where the air was tinged with the gentle scent of paint and varnish. Canvases lined the walls, each depicting vibrant scenes of winter landscapes and festive cheer. The colours seemed to leap from the surface, so vivid and full of life that Sophie felt as if she could step right into them.

"Your work is beautiful," she exclaimed.

One of the painters, an elf with a palette in one hand and a brush in the other, turned to her with a warm smile. "Thank you, dear. I am Elfangelo," he introduced himself, his voice carrying a slight Italian twang. His eyes twinkling beneath a cap dusted with flecks of paint. "We put our hearts into every brushstroke." With a flourish, he gave a little bow, then returned his focus to the canvas before him, where he continued to paint with graceful, sweeping motions. Elfangelo's brush danced across the surface, adding life to a snowy village scene complete with twinkling lights and laughing children. Sophie watched, fascinated by the way his movements translated into such exquisite details, capturing the essence of Christmas in each stroke. Around them, other elves worked diligently, their own styles unique but equally captivating. Some painted toys that would later bring joy to a child somewhere around the world, while others restored old toys to their former glory, ensuring each was as splendid as it had once been.

"This is more than just painting," Elfangelo explained without looking up, his voice soft yet filled with passion. "It's instilling each toy with a piece of our joy and Christmas spirit, so that when a child plays with one, they can feel the love and care that went into it."

Sophie nodded, deeply moved by the thought and care that these elves put into their work, making each toy not just a plaything, but a bearer of happiness, warmth and love.

As Santa's voice echoed through the bustling workshop, a chorus of cheerful greetings rose from the elves. They paused in their tasks, turning towards Sophie and Lily with bright smiles and twinkling eyes. The atmosphere, already lively, seemed to sparkle even more with the introduction of the girls.

"Hello, Sophie, hello Lily!" exclaimed an elf with a streak of blue paint on his cheek. He waved a brush in the air, leaving a trail of glittering specks. "Welcome to our workshop!"

Another elf busy adjusting a knitting pattern looked up and beamed. "It's so nice to meet Santa's special guests! My name is Elfadora." she said, her voice as melodious as the chimes hanging by her workstation. Santa gestured towards the knitting machine that captivated Lily's attention. "This is Elfred, the master of the knitting machine," he introduced. The elf, with a patterned cap perched jauntily on his head, bowed slightly. "I am pleased to meet you, Lily and Sophie. Each sweater is knitted with warmth and joy, hoping to bring comfort to its new owner."

As Santa led Sophie and Lily through the bustling workshop, every elf they encountered paused to greet them warmly; their faces alight with the joy of the season. The sound of cheerful Christmas tunes echoed softly in the background, creating a festive atmosphere. They passed the wrapping station, where an elf named Elftinsel, the overseer of the area, stood out prominently. Her nimble fingers moved in a blur, wrapping gifts with incredible speed and precision. The wrapping paper around her shimmered with vibrant colours and ribbons curled into perfect spirals.

"Each gift is a little bundle of happiness," Elftinsel explained, her eyes twinkling beneath her festive hat adorned with tiny jingling bells. Her workstation was a flurry of activity, with elves passing her boxes of various shapes and sizes. Despite the fast pace, each package she touched was meticulously adorned, showcasing her expert craftsmanship and dedication to spreading joy.

Lily and Sophie watched in awe as Elftinsel seamlessly selected papers and ribbons that matched the gifts, each choice thoughtful and deliberate. Her joyful demeanour and the loving attention she gave to each gift deeply impressed them, reinforcing the magic and love infused in every corner of the workshop.

"This is Elfanora," Santa introduced, pointing to another elf with a radiant smile, deftly spinning a ribbon into an elaborate bow. She was stationed nearby, her area was just as animated as Elftinsel's. "She's our chief gift-wrapper."

Elfanora waved at the girls, her hands never pausing. "Welcome to our wrapping wonderland!" she chimed, her voice as cheerful as the jingle of her bells. "Every ribbon, every bow, is tied with love."

Sophie leaned in closer, watching in awe. "How do you make it look so easy?" she asked, her eyes following Elfanora 's swift movements.

Elfanora laughed, a light, tinkling sound. "Years of practice and a sprinkle of elf magic," she replied. "Here, let me show you."

With a swift motion, she handed Sophie a ribbon and guided her hands in tying a simple but elegant bow. Sophie's face lit up with delight as she completed the bow under Elfanora's expert tutelage.

"Bravo!" Santa clapped, his eyes gleaming with mirth. "You're a natural, Sophie."

At the electronics assembly line, Lily and Sophie witnessed the fascinating process of constructing intricate electronic toys. The station was abuzz with elves and the soft whir of machines. An elf named Elfinstein, known for his expertise and meticulous work, stood at the forefront of this technological hub.

Elfinstein demonstrated how they assembled the toys, each component laid out with precision on his workstation. "It's like a puzzle, fitting all the parts together," he explained, his hands expertly connecting pieces of circuit boards, wires, and tiny mechanical parts. His fingers moved with deft assurance, as if each motion was second nature.

Above his station, detailed diagrams and blueprints were pinned up, showing the complex inner workings of toys that included everything from remote-controlled cars to programmable robots. Elfinstein picked up a small motor, a critical part of a toy helicopter, and seamlessly integrated it with the other components. "You see, each part has its place and role," he continued, "and when they all come together, they create something fun, something wonderful."

Lily and Sophie were captivated by the meticulous process, their faces lit up with curiosity as they watched each electronic toy come to life. The atmosphere was filled with a sense of accomplishment and pride, as each elf worked efficiently, guided by Elfinstein's expertise.

The girls were impressed by the dedication and skill of each elf. The love and care which went into every aspect of the toy-making process were evident in the joyful atmosphere and the perfection of each toy.

"They're true believers." Shouted an elf.

The elves erupted in applause, their faces beaming with admiration. "We're so happy to have you here!" they chorused, the workshop ringing with their joyful voices.

Santa motioned the girls to follow him,

As they did, Lily was drawn to the sound of laughter coming from a group of elves working on a particularly large gift. "What's happening here?" she inquired, her curiosity piqued.

"This is Elfstan," Santa introduced, nodding towards an elf wearing oversized spectacles, who was orchestrating the wrapping of the large gift. "He specialises in wrapping the more... unusual gifts."

Elfstan, with a mischievous glint in his eye, winked at Lily. "We elves love a good challenge," he said, gesturing towards the gift, which was almost as big as him. "This one's a bicycle for a very lucky child."

Lily watched as Elfstan and his team expertly navigated the wrapping process, their coordination and teamwork a sight to behold. "It's like watching a dance," she remarked, her voice filled with admiration.

Santa beamed at the girls. "Our elves take great pride in their work. Every gift which leaves this workshop carries with it the joy and hopes of Christmas."

In a brightly lit corner of Santa's expansive workshop, a number of elves meticulously inspected each toy and gift before it was cleared for wrapping and delivery. This area, buzzing with the hum of efficiency, was the quality control station, a critical checkpoint in the toy-making process. The elves, clad in neat uniforms with a magnifying glass looped around their necks, represented the last line of defence in ensuring the joy and safety of every child on Christmas morning.

With a keen eye, they examined each toy for any signs of defects: small splinters on wooden toys, loose threads on stuffed animals, or any mechanical issues in electronic gadgets. Their workspace was surrounded by bins labelled "Approved", "Minor Fixes", and "Major Repairs", organising the workflow and ensuring nothing was overlooked.

The quality control elves were trained to not only spot flaws but also to perform minor repairs on the spot. Equipped with a small toolkit, the elves could tighten a screw, sew up a tear, or smooth out a rough edge with practiced ease. For more complicated issues, they would send the toys to a specialised repair station where other skilled elves would work their magic. Sophie and Lily watched as these elves conducted random safety tests, simulating various conditions to ensure each toy could withstand enthusiastic play. They pulled, twisted, and even dropped items from heights to test their durability and ensure that all safety standards were met.

As they continued their tour, Sophie and Lily were introduced to more elves, each with their own unique role and personality. There was Elferoni, the jokester of the workshop, always ready with a witty quip, and Elfalina, who plays pranks on the un-expecting elves.

Santa turned to the girls and in a loud voice announced, "Who wants to see where we make the candy canes, peppermint cakes and gingerbread?"

Both girls raised their hands so quickly, their excitement was unmistakable. "Yes, please!" they exclaimed in unison, their eyes alight with anticipation.

Santa's booming laughter filled the space as he led Sophie and Lily towards another magical part of the North Pole, the food factory. As they approached, the sweet and spicy scents of Christmas treats wafted towards them, a delightful prelude to the wonders they were about to witness.

The door to the food factory opened, revealing a wonderland of culinary magic. The room was alive with a kaleidoscope of colours and bustling activity. Elves, adorned in candy-striped aprons, moved between ovens, mixers, and candy-making machines, their movements a well-orchestrated ballet of baking and confectionery art.

"This is where we make all the Christmas treats," Santa explained, his voice filled with pride. "Our elves are not only toy makers but master bakers and the creators of the very best sweets and toffees."

The first thing which caught Lily's attention was the candy cane machine. It was a marvel of engineering, with bright red and white stripes of candy being twisted, turned, and fed into a machine that turned out thousands of perfect canes all cut to the same size. The rhythmic motion of the machine was hypnotic, and the air around it was infused with the sharp, sweet scent of peppermint.

"Look at that!" Sophie pointed towards a group of elves decorating gingerbread houses. Each house was a masterpiece, decorated with intricate icing designs, gumdrops, and shimmering sugar snow. The smell of gingerbread was warm and inviting.

One of the elves, noticing their interest, waved them over. "Would you like to try decorating a gingerbread house?" she asked, her eyes twinkling with merriment.

Sophie's eyes widened with excitement. "We'd love to!"

Lily and Sophie were each given a gingerbread house and an array of colourful icings and sweets. They set to work, Lily's tongue poking out in concentration as she piped icing and placed sweets with care. The elves offered tips and encouragement, their laughter adding to the fun.

"I declare it a draw!" said the elf when they finished, congratulating them both.

Nearby, another machine drew their attention, the peppermint cake maker. This machine was a symphony of moving parts and steam whistles, where layers of cake were assembled, frosted, and sprinkled with crushed peppermint. The result was a visually stunning and aromatic masterpiece which made the girls' mouths water.

"Would you like a taste?" an elf asked, slicing a small piece from a freshly made cake. Both girls nodded eagerly, and upon tasting, their faces lit up with delight. The cake was a perfect blend of ginger and marzipan flavours combining in a light and fluffy texture.

"Everything tastes amazing!" Lily exclaimed, her eyes shining with joy.

"It's like a dream come true," Sophie added, savouring the last crumbs of her slice of cake.

Santa watched them with a contented smile. "Christmas is a time of joy and sharing, and what better way to spread joy than with sweet treats made right here at the North Pole."

As they continued to explore the food factory, they encountered more enchanting sights, a chocolate fountain where elves dipped various fruits and marshmallows, as they watched one mischievous elf pushed another elf's head under the flowing chocolate. Lily and Sophie's burst into fits of giggles. There was a machine which spun sugar into delicate threads to create candyfloss clouds, and an area where elves hand-painted intricate designs on lollipops.

Each workstation was a fantastic blend of tradition and innovation. The air was filled with laughter, the clatter of utensils, and the heartwarming scents of baking.

As their tour of the food factory came to an end, Sophie and Lily knew they'd experienced something truly special. They had not only seen the magic of Christmas in the making of toys but also tasted it in the form of delicious treats crafted by the talented elves.

139

"Thank you, Santa, for showing us this magical place," Sophie said, her voice filled with gratitude.

"And thank you to all the elves," Lily added. "You've made our Christmas even more special."

Leaving the food factory, Santa turned to them, "The tour is not over yet." He smiled and winked, "We have not seen the letter sorting area."

Santa guided Sophie and Lily through a maze of festive corridors, their steps echoing with excitement. As they approached the letter sorting area, the sound of fluttering paper and gentle murmurs of reading filled the air. The room they entered was bathed in a warm, golden glow, emanating from letter sorting devices. The walls were lined with shelves overflowing with envelopes of every size and colour.

"This is the second letter sorting area," Santa said, his voice filled with a reverence that matched the seriousness of the room. Elves, perched at long wooden tables, were engrossed in the task of sorting through thousands of letters. Each elf had a kindly face and a gentle smile, carefully opening envelopes, their eyes twinkling as they read the contents.

Sophie and Lily watched in amazement as some of the letters seemed to sort themselves into neat piles, as if by magic. "How do they do that?" Sophie whispered, her eyes wide with wonder.

Santa chuckled softly. "Ah, a little bit of elf magic and a lot of Christmas spirit. Each letter finds its place, ensuring no wish is overlooked."

The girls observed as one elf, with rosy cheeks, read a letter aloud. "Dear Santa, I wish for a red bike and a skateboard," he recited. The other elves paused in their work, nodding in agreement before resuming their task with renewed vigour.

Lily leaned in closer, captivated by the scene. "It's amazing," she remarked, her voice filled with delight.

Santa guided them to a corner of the room, where an intricate machine whirred softly. The machine, trimmed with gears and levers, magically scanned the letters, its lights blinking in a rhythmic dance. "This is the Dream Weaver," Santa explained. "It helps us categorise the wishes based on urgency, type, and location."

An elf with spectacles perched on the tip of his nose approached them, a bright smile on his face. "I'm Elford, keeper of the Dream Weaver," he said, extending a hand. "It's a pleasure to meet Santa's special guests."

Sophie and Lily greeted Elford, their eyes still fixed on the machine. "It's amazing," Sophie said.

Elford beamed with pride. "It's one of our most important tools. It ensures every child's wish is heard and considered."

As they continued their tour, the girls were struck by the care and attention each elf gave to the letters. The room resonated with the sound of paper rustling, soft laughter, and the occasional exclamation of delight.

"Each of these letters represents a child's hope," Santa said, gazing fondly at his team of elves. "It's our job to make as many as possible come true."

"We have one more stop before it is time to get ready to leave. Can you guess where we are going now?"

Both girls looked at each other and shrugged. "We've seen how the toys are made and wrapped. We've been to the food factory, seen the letters." pondered Sophie.

"What about delivery?" said Santa with a smile, "We can't deliver all these presents without the reindeer."

"The reindeer, of course!" exclaimed Lily.

"You saw them and the sleigh yesterday as we flew over the North Pole, now we can go and get a closer look at the reindeer. I can also show you how the magic of the sleigh works."

"You better fasten up your coats, we are going outside. It can be a bit nippy this time of year." Joked Santa.

With their coats fastened snugly against the crisp Arctic air, Sophie and Lily followed Santa through the crunching snow, their breath forming little clouds in the frosty air. The anticipation of meeting the legendary reindeer made their hearts beat faster, and their eyes shine with excitement.

As they approached the reindeer compound, a grand structure of polished wood and sparkling lights came into view. The compound, vast and sprawling, was bordered by tall fences adorned with twinkling fairy lights and garlands of evergreen. The air was filled with the earthy scent of pine along with the subtle musk of the reindeer, creating a rustic yet inviting atmosphere.

"Here we are," Santa announced, his voice filled with affection. "The home of my trusted reindeer."

The gates to the compound swung open, revealing a spacious area dotted with cosy-looking stables and large open areas covered in a blanket of snow. The reindeer, magnificent creatures with lush, glossy coats and grand antlers, were lounging, grazing, or playfully frolicking in the snow. Their fur glistened in the soft light, their colours ranging from deep browns to dappled greys, each reindeer unique in its splendour.

Sophie gasped in awe. "They're beautiful!"

"Indeed, they are," Santa agreed, a proud smile on his face. "Each one plays a vital role in our Christmas journey."

An elf, dressed in a warm, fur-lined coat and sunglasses, approached them. "Welcome to the reindeer compound," he greeted. "I'm Elfis, the reindeer caretaker."

Elfis led them closer to the reindeer, who regarded them with gentle, curious eyes. The girls reached out tentatively, and to their delight, the reindeer nuzzled their hands, their breath warm and slightly ticklish.

"This is Dasher," Elfis introduced, pointing to a lively reindeer playfully bounding through the snow. "And over there is Dancer," he continued, indicating a graceful reindeer skipping elegantly.

As they walked through the compound, they were introduced to each of Santa's famed reindeer. Vixen, with her intelligent eyes and sleek coat, Prancer, with his energetic leaps. "The reindeer train all year for Christmas Eve," Elfis explained. "They need to be in top shape to fly around the world."

Lily, her eyes following a reindeer as it galloped across the field, asked, "Do they ever get tired?"

Elfis chuckled. "They're magical creatures. They have stamina like no other, but we make sure they're well-rested and cared for."

The compound was alive with the sounds of the reindeer's gentle huffs and the crunching of snow under their hooves. The air was crisp and invigorating; it pinched at the girls rosy cheeks.

Santa gathered the girls close. "These reindeer are more than just animals; they're a symbol of the Christmas spirit, resilient, joyful, and full of wonder."

Santa led Lily and Sophie to the sleigh, its polished wooden frame gleaming. The plush seats looked even more inviting now, and the golden runners shimmered as if they were infused with stardust. Every inch of the sleigh seemed to radiate a quiet magic, one that whispered of countless journeys across moonlit skies.

"Come closer, girls," Santa beckoned, his eyes twinkling. "There's something special I'd like to show you."

He pointed to a small, ornate object at the front of the sleigh. A golden compass, round and gleaming, was pulsating with a strange light. It wasn't like any compass Lily or Sophie had seen before. Instead of pointing north, its needle spun slowly, occasionally stopping and glowing brightly before continuing its lazy rotation. Around its edge, tiny, intricate symbols shifted and shimmered, changing with every movement of the needle.

"This," Santa said, "is my magic compass. It's one of the most important tools I have."

Lily leaned in, her eyes wide with wonder. "But... how does it work?"

Santa chuckled softly, "Ah, that's the secret, my dear. You see, this compass doesn't just point north. It points to the hearts of children all over the world who believe in the magic of Christmas. It guides me to every single home, no matter where they are, even those that seem hidden or far away."

Sophie's mouth dropped open as she stared at the glowing compass. "So, that's how you find your way in the dark?"

"Exactly," Santa nodded. "It's more than just a tool for navigation. The compass bends time and space, allowing me to travel faster than the wind, faster than a heartbeat, so that I can deliver every single present in just one night. When I follow its light, the sleigh becomes weightless, and time slows down, allowing me to visit each child without a moment wasted."

He paused, letting the girls take in the enormity of what he was saying. "That's why I never get lost, no matter how far I travel. As long as there's someone who believes in Christmas, the compass will always guide me to them."

Lily reached out a hand, hesitating just before touching it. "It's beautiful," she whispered. "And it's... warm?"

"Yes," Santa agreed. "It's warmed by the belief and love that children all over the world have for Christmas. That's the real magic, you see. It's not the sleigh, or the reindeer, or even me, it's the spirit of Christmas that powers it all."

Sophie and Lily, their hearts warmed by the encounter, waved goodbye to the reindeer, each with a newfound appreciation for these majestic creatures.

"Thank you for showing us this, Santa," Sophie said, her voice filled with gratitude.

"It's been incredible," Lily added, her eyes still fixed on the reindeer.

As they made their way back to Santa's house, the image of the reindeer, strong and serene against the winter backdrop, would be a lasting memory. They not only met Santa Claus and his elves, but they also came face to face with the magic of Christmas, embodied in the gentle eyes and noble antlers of the reindeer of the North Pole.

Chapter 12

Walking back to the main house, the girls were quiet, each lost in their own thoughts. The North Pole workshops were more than they could have ever imagined. That afternoon, as they sat by the crackling fire, sipping hot chocolate and reflecting on their adventure, Lily turned to Sophie. "I'll never look at a Christmas present the same way again," she said, her voice filled with wonder.

Sophie nodded in agreement. "This Christmas is truly special, it's definitely a Christmas to remember."

Jingles ran into the living room, Santa was sat with the girls enjoying a hot chocolate before the big night. "The magic compass, it's gone!" he exclaimed, his brows furrowed in worry. "Without it, we can't navigate tonight; no one will get their presents."

Lily and Sophie turned to each other, a sense of urgency building within them. "We have to help find it," Lily whispered, determination lighting up her eyes.

Sophie nodded, "Where do we start looking?"

"Let's start where it was last seen," Santa suggested. "It can't be that far away."

Together, with Santa leading the way, they entered the stables where the sleigh is kept. The sleigh, a magnificent vessel of red and gold, sat idle. The compass had always been securely fastened to its dashboard, guiding Santa through the skies with its enchanted glow and magical properties.

"Let's think like detectives," Sophie said, her gaze sweeping over the room. "Where could it have gone?"

They began their search, examining every nook and cranny. Some of the elves even joined in, their faces etched with concern. The compass wasn't just a tool; it was part of the magic by which the sleigh travelled so fast.

As they searched, Lily noticed a trail of sparkling dust leading away from the sleigh. "Look at this," she called out. The trail meandered across the floor, disappearing under a pile of gift sacks.

Kneeling down, Sophie carefully moved the sacks aside. Beneath them, they found a curious sight, a group of tiny, mischievous elves known as the Tinkerers, who were usually responsible for repairs.

"What are you doing here?" Santa asked.

"We were playing hide and seek," one of the Tinkerers confessed, his cheeks turning a rosy shade of red.

"Have you seen my compass? My magic compass. I cannot use the sleigh without it. Tonight being Christmas eve night, all the children will be getting excited about their gifts, imagine how disappointed they will be when there are none under the tree." Santa sounded concerned.

"No Santa, we have not seen it. This is not good." One of the Tinkerers replied.

"Could it have come loose and rolled away somewhere?" Asked Lily.

Santa shook his head. "It's possible, but the compass isn't just an ordinary object. It's infused with magic; it shouldn't just pop out of its housing and roll away on its own."

Word had spread to the workshops. Usually a place of cheerful activity, but now they were clouded with an air of mystery and concern. Elves paused in their work, their expressions reflecting the gravity of the situation. The magic compass was the heart of Christmas Eve's operation, its loss a potential catastrophe.

Lily and Sophie, realising the seriousness of the matter, decided to take a more investigative approach. "Let's think about this," Sophie proposed. "We need to think about who would have been here last and why the compass might have been taken."

They started by interviewing the elves who had been working near the sleigh. One by one, the elves recounted their activities, but none had seen the compass or noticed anything unusual.

As they continued their inquiries, Lily noticed an elf standing apart from the others, her gaze shifting nervously. "Let's talk to her," she whispered to Sophie.

Approaching the elf, who introduced herself as Tinseltoes, they asked if he had seen anything suspicious. After a moment of hesitation, Tinseltoes spoke up. "I did see Glitterstep near the sleigh earlier. She seemed hurried and... Concerned about something."

"Glitterstep?" Santa mused, as he stroked his beard. "But she's one of our most dedicated elves. It doesn't make sense."

Deciding to follow this new lead, Santa, accompanied by Lily and Sophie, went to find her. They found her in the wrapping department, her hands shaking slightly as she tied a ribbon.

"Glitterstep, we need to ask you about the magic compass," Santa said gently. "Tinseltoes mentioned seeing you near the sleigh earlier."

Glitterstep's eyes widened, and for a moment, she looked like she might start crying. But then, with a deep sigh, she nodded. "Yes, I was there. I saw the compass, but I didn't take it. I was worried about it, though. I overheard two of the Tinkerers talking about taking the compass apart to see how it works. I was going to tell you, Santa, but I didn't want to cause any trouble."

Santa's expression softened. "Thank you for owning up, Glitterstep. It's important to speak up when something isn't right."

Armed with this new information, Santa, Lily, and Sophie returned to question the Tinkerers again. This time, the Tinkerers looked at each other nervously, the guilt evident by their fidgeting hands.

Finally, one Tinkerer, Blink, stepped forward. "It was me. I took the compass. I wanted to understand how it worked, to see the magic inside. But then it started glowing strangely, different to its normal glow and moving on its own, and I got scared. I didn't know what to do, so I hid it."

"Where is it now, Blink?" Santa asked, his tone firm but not unkind.

Blink led them to a small, hidden compartment behind a workbench. There, nestled among a pile of gears and wires, lay the magic compass. Its surface glowed with a soft, pulsing green light, its needle spinning erratically.

Santa picked up the compass, examining it closely. "It seems to be damaged, but we'll have to run some tests to be sure."

147

Santa's brows furrowed as he carefully turned the magic compass in his hands, its usual steady glow now flickering with uncertainty. The workshop, normally alive with the sounds of merriment and industry, had fallen into a tense hush. Elves peeked from behind workstations, their expressions a mix of concern and curiosity.

"Santa, what will we do if it can't be fixed?" Sophie asked, her voice filled with concern.

"I know someone who just might be able to help." Said Tinseltoes.

"Ticktock!" exclaimed Blink.

In a flash of blue sparkles, Jingles appeared with Ticktock.

"Ah, Ticktock. I have an important job for you." Santa, normally a beacon of joviality, his features now etched with a sense of seriousness as he handed the critical compass to Ticktock. He carefully inspected the compass, "Hmm, I need my special tools for this." he said as he headed off to his workstation, followed by Santa, Jingles and the girls.

As Ticktock, the master clock mender of the North Pole, approached his workbench, the air around him thickened with a sense of foreboding. Every eye in Santa's workshop was fixed on him, their collective breaths held in a tense suspension. The stakes had never been higher; Christmas itself seemed to balance precariously on the edge of uncertainty.

The very essence of Christmas magic seemed to have faltered, a fact that made the usually vibrant workshop feel as though it were shrouded in a thin veil of gloom.

Ticktock, whose reputation for repairing the unrepairable was known far and wide, cradled the compass with a reverence that spoke volumes of its importance. His tiny workshop, usually a haven of ticking clocks and whirring gears, now felt like the centre stage of a drama.

"I'll do my best, Santa. I understand how vital this is," Ticktock assured with a nod, but as he turned to his cluttered workspace filled with gears, springs, and an array of mysterious tools, doubt seemed to creep into every corner of the room. The walls, lined with clocks of every size, ticked in unison, as if counting down the moments to a critical deadline.

As he began his work, Ticktock's hands moved with a precision born of decades of practice, yet his usual confident demeanour was replaced with a furrowed brow, deep in concentration. A bead of sweat trickled down his forehead, reflecting the faint light from the overhead lamps. The usual cheerful clinks and clatters of his tools were now overshadowed by a heavy silence that seemed to echo with the weight of his task.

The other elves exchanged worried glances, their festive hats and bright aprons doing little to ward off the feeling of uncertainty that settled over them. Ticktock's every adjustment, every tightening of a screw, and every calibration was watched with bated breath.

Minutes ticked by, feeling more like hours, as Ticktock's skilled hands worked tirelessly. However, a heavy sigh eventually escaped him, causing a ripple of anxiety to spread through the onlookers.

"It cannot be used, it is broken. As it stands, it is useless." he murmured, the gravity of his words sinking into the hearts of the elves and dimming the usual festive lights of the workshop.

"The magic core has destabilised," he announced gravely. "It's a delicate procedure, but I think I can stabilise it. However, the realignment will require a rare element only found in the deepest mines of the North Pole."

Santa's face grew thoughtful. "The Starlite crystals," he murmured. "But mining them is risky as they are so delicate, and we have so little time."

Sophie stepped forward, determination in her voice. "Let us help, Santa. We can go to the mines. We can't just stand here and do nothing."

Santa looked at the girls, the resolve in their eyes matching his own. "It's arduous, but I believe in you. You've shown great courage and resourcefulness recently."

Santa speedily assembled a team of his most skilled elves to accompany Lily and Sophie on their perilous journey to the mines. The urgency of their mission hung heavily over them as they donned headlamps, clutched their pickaxes, and layered on warm clothing. They set off on sleds pulled by an eager pack of Huskie dogs, their excited barks showing they were impatient to get started, breath's misting in the frigid air. The Arctic twilight cast a surreal light over the landscape, the sky swirling with greens, pinks, and purples.

The path to the mines was treacherous, winding through snow-laden fields and jagged, icy caverns. The sleds bumped and slid across the uneven terrain, threatening to veer off course at every turn. Their huskies panted heavily, their eyes gleaming in the dim light, pressing onward through the biting cold with a sense of urgency.

As they neared the mines, the temperature plummeted, a chill gnawing at their fingers and toes, seeping into their very bones. The wind howled through the barren expanse, whipping their faces with icy shards. The dark opening of the mine loomed ahead, an ominous gaping void in the endless whiteness.

Sophie's breath came in shallow puffs, her eyes wide as she stared into the abyss. "Are we ready for this?" she asked, her voice wavering, barely audible above the whistling wind.

Lily squeezed her arm, her own face pale against the dark backdrop. "We have to be," she replied, her words a reminder of their mission's urgency. "For the Johannson family, and for all those who need us."

The determined elves huddled together, their faces showing unwavering resolve. They knew the journey ahead would test them, but their resolve was unshakable. They exchanged a final nod before collectively taking a deep breath. Stepping forward, they entered the cold and ominous depths of the mine. The darkness engulfed them completely, as they speedily turned on their torches.

The chamber inside was like a frozen dreamscape, with walls covered in glittering crystals. These icy facets caught the light and shattered it into a rainbow of colours. The colours danced and played upon the walls like a kaleidoscope, twisting and twirling, creating a mesmerising and ever-changing display. The light fragments shimmered and flickered, creating a dazzling show. They navigated the narrow passages, their breaths echoing in the stillness.

Finally, Lily and Sophie, guided by the elves and the faint flicker of torchlight, reached the cavern where the Starlite crystals grew. A hushed awe fell over them as they entered, the air thick with a sense of magic. High above in the rocky walls, embedded like jewels in an earthen crown, the crystals glowed with an ethereal green light. Their faint luminescence pulsated gently, casting eerie shadows that danced along the craggy surfaces, starkly contrasting the encompassing darkness. The silence in the cavern was intense, broken only by the distant drip of water, each echo a haunting reminder of the isolation and depth of their subterranean location. There was an unnerving sense of being watched, shadows seeming to shift with a life of their own as if the cave itself was aware of their intrusion.

With hearts pounding in the eerie quiet, Lily and Sophie approached the walls cautiously. The tiny crystals' glow, though mesmerising, carried an undertone of forewarning, as if the cavern guarded its treasures jealously. Despite the urgency of their mission to restore the magic compass with these crystals, the chill in the air seemed to whisper caution. Their hands, though steady, were cold as they began the delicate task of extracting the tiny Starlite crystals. Each crystal had to be carefully dislodged from its ancient perch, a process fraught with risk as the slightest mishap could shatter the precious gem, its energy vital not just for the compass, but possibly, they feared, for their safe return. The crystals hummed softly, the energy an unmistakable force that felt almost awake.

As they worked, the cave seemed to press in closer around them, the darkness deepening, the air growing colder. Finally the elves had safely dislodged a couple of the crystals intact. This delicate operation, under such an oppressive atmosphere, tested their courage as much as their skill, for every moment spent in that mysterious cavern weighed heavily upon their spirits, a constant reminder of the fine line they trod between success and failure.

With the crystals secured in their backpack, they hurried back through the mines, the weight of their task propelling them forward. They made their way back to the workshop as speedily as they could. Ticktock eagerly awaited their return. With the Starlite crystals in hand, he set to work on the compass. The elves, Lily, and Sophie gathered around, watching as he delicately placed the crystal into the compass. He carefully screwed it back together and turned it over to view the pointer needle. Nothing, it wasn't moving. He gave it a very gentle shake, again, nothing. Ticktock let out a deep gasp, looked at Santa and gently shook his head. He placed the Compass on his workbench, a defeated look upon his face. Whispers of his failure to repair the magic compass spread across the workshop.

"At least you gave it your best shot." Said Santa as his head dropped and his shoulders sank.

"Those poor children what are we going to do now?" Asked Lily.

Santa shook his head slowly, "That I don't know. Christmas may not happen this year girls."

The girls looked at each other; their hearts sank as their eyes welled up with tears. The workshop became still, the elves looked at each other, as one by one their faces saddened. The stillness hung heavy in the workshop, the sense of defeat settling like a cold blanket over everyone. The once cheerful sounds of hammering and laughter had now faded, replaced by soft murmurs of despair. Even the twinkling lights seemed to dim, their glow no longer bright and cheerful but dull, as if they too had lost hope. Santa stood there, his broad shoulders slumped in a way that made him seem smaller, almost fragile. Lily and Sophie clung to each other, their eyes wet with tears. All around them, elves wiped at their own eyes, trying to be brave but failing. The magic, it seemed, had disappeared from this most magical place on earth. Ticktock remained by the workbench, staring down at the compass, as if willing it to work, to give them just one sign that all wasn't lost. He sighed deeply, shaking his head, tears ran down his face as he began to turn away.

Something caught his eye, the compass flashed. Slowly, the compass began to glow steadily once again, its light brightening until it shone like a miniature star. The needle, which had been motionless started to align itself once more.

A cheer erupted from the elves, relief and joy washing over them in waves. Santa, his eyes moist with gratitude, embraced Lily and Sophie. "You've done it, girls, you've done it.

Ticktock, you have just saved Christmas," he said, his voice thick with emotion. "You've saved Christmas."

The workshop burst into activity once more, the elves once more invigorated by the restored magic. The sleigh was prepared, the reindeer harnessed, and the sacks of presents started to be loaded.

As the elves prepared Santa's annual journey, Santa turned to Lily and Sophie. "You two are more than just honorary elves, you really are both extra special elves in my book. You're both heroes of Christmas. Thank you for believing, and for never giving up."

As the early evening sky deepened to a rich twilight blue, dusted with the first twinkling stars, and the Northern Lights began their dance across the sky, Santa invited the girls for a last cup of hot peppermint chocolate. They sat in his cosy study, the fire crackling merrily in the hearth.

"You two have shown great initiative and bravery today," Santa said, handing each of them each a steaming mug of chocolate.

The girls exchanged excited glances, their faces glowing in the firelight. "Thank you, Santa," Lily said, her voice warm with happiness. "This has been the best adventure ever. This is certainly a Christmas to remember."

Sophie nodded in agreement, her eyes sparkling. "We'll never forget this day."

Lily and Sophie looked around Santa's study, surrounded by shelves filled with ancient books titled 'Naughty list' and 'Nice list'. They sat comfortably in deep, velvet cushions on their armchairs. Outside, the stars above shimmered softly, guardians of the evening's dreams.

Sophie looked at Santa, her face betrayed the burning desire to ask him a question, "Santa, have you ever been caught delivering presents?"

"I have come close to being seen on a few occasions, but I always managed to avoid it." He said, smiling warmly.

"Can you tell us about some please? And, how you built your workshops." Sophies eyes lit up in anticipation.

"Let me tell you about the workshops first." Santa began, placing his mug aside; let me tell you how the North Pole Workshops came to be."

In the snug embrace of Santa's study, the night outside wrapping the world with whispers of Christmas. Lily and Sophie gave their full attention, eager for the tale that was about to unfold. Santa's voice, rich and comforting, filled the room as he embarked on his story.

Lily and Sophie leaned in, captivated, their eyes wide with wonder as Santa recounted the enchanting tale of how he summoned the elves to erect the very first Christmas workshop. "You see, children," Santa began, his voice soft against the crackling of the fire, "summoning the elves was no ordinary task. It required not only a call but a heartfelt incantation, for elves are creatures not just of this realm but of an enchantment woven through the very fabric of the dream world."

Santa lifted his hands as if holding an invisible delicate thread between them. "In the deepest silence of that frosty night, under the silver glow of the moon, I crafted a charm from the essence of the North Pole itself, the purity of the snow, the whisper of the winter wind, and the resilience of the evergreens. Into this charm, I wove my dreams for a Christmas where every child felt the joy and love of the season."

He paused, his eyes twinkling in the low light, a secretive smile playing at the corners of his lips. In a flash, he was holding a small, golden Christmas wreath charm. It was no bigger than his thumbnail.

"Then, I recited an ancient Elvish chant, a melody so old and so sweet that no human ear has fully grasped its beauty. The wind carried the tune across the icy plains, through the silvery forests, and into the hidden enclaves of the dream world were elves' dwell. As the melody echoed through the North Pole, it reached the ears of the elves, stirring them from their winter tasks. Drawn to the sound and the magic of the charm, they came in droves, their eyes alight with curiosity and their hearts ready to embrace a new adventure. They travelled by starlight, sliding over the ice, tiptoeing through the snow, their laughter like the tinkling of tiny bells."

"Upon their arrival, they found the charm I left in the heart of a clearing, pulsing with a warm, inviting glow. The elves, understanding the call of duty and the dream interwoven with their summoning, immediately set to work. Their hands were nimble, their spirits high; they sang songs of ancient elfish folklore as they built, infusing the workshop with magic that is both ancient and new."

Santa's eyes gleamed with pride as he continued. "It was constructed, as I said, not merely from timber and nails, but from unabated love, boundless dreams, and, of course, a generous dash of Christmas magic."

"But why the North Pole?" asked Sophie.

Santa's eyes sparkled with amusement at Sophie's question, a chuckle escaping him as if it were a shared secret between old friends. "Ah, that's an excellent question," he said, leaning back in his chair, the leather creaking softly under his weight. "The North Pole is unique, not just because it's the top of the world, but because it's a place where magic can thrive unhindered by the outside world. It's a place where time seems to stand still under this dome of invisibility, allowing us to prepare for Christmas with the utmost care and dedication."

He paused, gazing into the fire as if the flames held memories. "The cold here is not just a barrier to the outside; it's a reminder of the warmth that Christmas brings to hearts around the world. And the isolation? It helps keep the magic of Christmas safe and pure, untainted by the rush and bustle of the modern world."

Lily and Sophie nodded, understanding dawning in their eyes. The choice of the North Pole wasn't just practical; it was symbolic, proof of the enduring spirit of Christmas that thrived in the harshest conditions, reminding everyone of the power of hope and joy.

"Plus," Santa added with a twinkle in his eye, "The reindeer love the snow."

As they sipped their hot chocolate, Santa leaned forward, his eyes twinkling with the reflection of the firelight, ready to impart a tale of when he was nearly caught delivering gifts. "One Christmas Eve, not so long ago, I found myself in quite a predicament," he began, his voice low and inviting, drawing Lily and Sophie into the heart of his story.

"I was in a small town in Norway, a beautiful place covered in a thick blanket of snow. It was past midnight, and all was going as planned, until I reached a particularly tricky house. This house had a chimney so narrow, I had to suck in my belly and wriggle down like an earthworm," Santa chuckled, his belly shaking like a bowl full of jelly.

Lily's eyes widened. "Did you get stuck?" she asked, the image of Santa wriggling down a chimney filling her with a mix of concern and amusement.

Santa nodded, his eyes gleaming with mirth. "Indeed, I did. For a moment, I thought I'd have to call on the elves to pull me out. But that wasn't the worst part. As I finally popped out of the fireplace, I heard a sound which made my heart skip a beat, the soft padding of little feet on the staircase."

Sophie gasped. "A child was coming?"

"Yes," Santa continued. "A little boy, six years old was coming down to check if I had visited. Thinking quickly, I did what I had to do... I hid behind the sofa, barely daring to breathe."

The girls leaned in closer, hanging on to every word. "Did he see you?" Lily whispered.

Santa shook his head. "Luckily, he didn't. He saw the presents under the tree, and with a satisfied smile, went back upstairs to wake his parents and tell them I had been and delivered everyone's presents. That was one of my closest calls."

The fire crackled in the hearth, casting a warm glow on their faces. Santa's stories transporting them to a world of midnight escapes, magical moments, and the joy of delivering happiness across the globe.

Among others he recounted a tale from a Christmas in Brazil. "It was a particularly warm Christmas Eve," Santa began. "I was delivering presents and as I entered an apartment through a window, since not many houses had chimneys there, I didn't realise there was a parrot in the room."

"A parrot?" Sophie asked, her eyes sparkling with curiosity.

156

"Yes, a very talkative one. As soon as I stepped in, it started squawking, 'Santa! Santa!', loud enough to wake the whole neighbourhood. I had to gently coax it with some carrot sticks I carry for the reindeer to snack on."

Lily laughed. "You must always be prepared for anything."

Santa nodded sagely. "Indeed, Lily. Being Santa requires a lot of quick thinking."

As the night deepened and their mugs emptied of the peppermint chocolate, Santa's stories drew to a close. "Now, girls," he said, his voice warm and soft, "it's time for you to get back home."

Right on cue, Jingles entered the room. "Time to go girls."

The girls stood up, disappointment written all over their faces, "It's sad we have to leave but we have had such a fantastic time. Thank you, Santa, thank you, Jingles." Said Lily.

"Thank you for everything." Sophie said as she approached Santa and gave him a big, warm hug."

Santa hugged her back then held his arms open as Lily rushed forward to hug him too. Santa looked at the girls and smiled, "Time here at the North Pole, and especially here at my workshop, passes differently to normal time. When Jingles takes you back, it will be time to get up on Christmas eve."

Lily and Sophie looked at each other in disbelief, "I don't understand?" said Lily.

"This is how I can deliver all these presents in one night, my magic sleigh, my magic compass and my particularly fast reindeer can slip through time in a flash. It's now time for you to go and enjoy Christmas eve with your families."

With a final wave goodbye, Jingles clicked his fingers. Lily and Sophie kept their eyes on Santa as the room faded in a swirl of twinkling magical lights. They were once more transported through the dazzling light of the magical vortex. As the vibrant hues of the vortex faded, Lily and Sophie found themselves back in the familiar surroundings of Lily's bedroom, the sense of wonder from their North Pole adventure lingered in the air. They glanced around, half-expecting Jingles to appear with a jingle of his bell, but the room remained still, bathed in the soft, early morning light of Christmas Eve. As they stood there, Lily and Sophie's eyes were drawn to Lily's bed, where an assortment of special gifts had mysteriously appeared. The realisation that these were parting gifts from the North Pole brought smiles to their faces, rekindling the magic of their adventure.

On the bed lay beautifully wrapped boxes of peppermint chocolate, the same kind they had savoured with Santa, each packet tied with a shimmering red ribbon. Beside them were candy canes, their red and white stripes glinting in the morning light, looking like miniature magical walking sticks. And there, in the centre, was a large, intricately decorated ginger and marzipan cake, its frosting glistening as if dusted with frost from the North Pole itself.

Sophie picked up a box of the peppermint chocolate. "Santa remembered how much we liked this," she said, her voice filled with a mix of surprise and delight.

Lily, holding one of the candy canes, added, "And these must be from the elves.

The girls marvelled at the thoughtfulness of the gifts, each item a reminder of their extraordinary journey. They knew these were not just ordinary treats; they were symbols of the magic and wonder they had experienced.

Outside, the world was waking up to Christmas Eve, unaware of the magical journey two young girls had just returned from. But in Lily's bedroom, the magic was very much alive, lingering in the air like the sweet scent of gingerbread and chocolate, a reminder of the true spirit of Christmas.

Lily, her eyes still sparkling from the adventure, turned to Sophie. "Can you believe it? We were actually at the North Pole!"

Sophie, sitting on the edge of Lily's bed, nodded, a mix of amazement and nostalgia in her voice. "It feels like a dream. But it was all real, wasn't it?"

They looked at each other, smiles spreading across their faces, and in unison shouted, "We met Santa!" as they danced around the room.

The girls, still in their warm clothes from the North Pole, decided to change and freshen up, their minds alive with the memories of their extraordinary journey. As they dressed, they recounted their favourite moments, Seeing where the toys were made, meeting the reindeer, and of course, the stories shared by Santa himself.

"Do you think anyone will believe us?" Lily wondered aloud as she pulled on her sweater.

Sophie, looking thoughtful, replied, "I don't know, I don't see why not, we have brought Christmas magic to the village. But we'll always have the memories, and that's what matters most."

Their conversation was interrupted by the sound of Lily's family stirring downstairs. The aroma of fresh pancakes wafting up to the room, a reminder it was indeed Christmas Eve, a day of joy and family celebrations.

"Come on," Lily said, excitement creeping into her voice. "Let's go and enjoy Christmas Eve!"

As Lily and Sophie made their way downstairs. The kitchen was a hive of activity, alive with the bustling sounds of Lily's family engrossed in festive preparations. The air was rich with the scent of mince pies baking in the oven, mingling with the laughter and chatter that filled the room.

"Merry Christmas Eve!" greeted Lily's mother, her face alight with a warm, welcoming smile. "You girls are up early. Did you sleep well? How was the North Pole?"

Lily and Sophie exchanged a knowing glance, their eyes sparkling with the remnants of last night's adventure. "It happened, it really happened," Sophie replied. The twinkle in her eye mirrored the fairy lights strung up around the room. "We visited the North Pole and met Santa."

"Sounds like you had quite the dream," said Lily's father with a hearty chuckle, flipping pancakes on the stovetop.

The girls shared a smile, their secret a precious bond they knew only they could fully understand. "It was the best dream," Lily affirmed, her voice brimming with contentment and wonder.

Later that morning, wrapped up in their warmest coats and scarves, Lily, and Sophie ventured into the village. As they walked the familiar paths, they noticed a subtle but definitive transformation. Villagers, who once passed each other with nothing more than a nod, were now greeting one another with smiles and warm wishes. The once reserved and less sociable residents engaged in lively conversations, their faces bright with Christmas cheer. The Winter Garden of Lights had a lasting impact on the people, spreading kindness and unity.

As the day wore on, Lily and Sophie, their hearts full of joy, as their village celebrated the most magical Christmas Eve. Under the glow of the festive lights, the girls knew that the true magic of Christmas lay not just in dreams, but in the shared joy and renewed bonds of their community. This, they understood, was the real magic of Christmas, enduring, transformative, and as real as the smiles on their neighbours' faces.

Sophie turned to Lily, "This certainly is a Christmas to Remember."

Every Christmas Eve from then onwards, the villagers honour Oliver's legacy before leading the Starlight Procession, which always culminates in the now-famous Winter Garden of Lights. Word of the village's transformation has spread, drawing people from far and wide to witness the magic.

Visitors from across the country flocked to the village to see its enchanting transformation. This once quiet village, revitalised by the spirit of Christmas and the visionary dreams of two young girls, now thrived as a bustling hub of life and laughter.